"I didn't think you believed in spontaneous human combustion," Dyson said to Slick.

"I've never seen a case," the M.E. explained. "But given the apparently legitimate sources of a number of reports, I'm willing to keep an open mind on the subject. On the other hand, all reported cases that I found in my research earlier this morning indicate that the source of the fire is internal."

"And that isn't the case here," Jenna said, understanding at last. "The muscles were barely touched by the flames, and even the skin was only badly charred on the outside."

"True. In fact, one of the victims died of cardiac failure. Likely brought on by the trauma of being burned."

"But wait a minute," Dyson put in, frowning. "If the burns were all external . . ."

"Then the source of the fire was external. Which means it was either a freak accident of some kind, or else a murder," Slick finished.

"But there are witnesses. There was no source for the flame. It just . . . happened," Jenna protested. "How can that be?"

Body of Evidence **thrillers**
by Christopher Golden

Body Bags
Thief of Hearts
Soul Survivor
Meets the Eye
Head Games
Skin Deep

with Rick Hautala
Burning Bones
Brain Trust
(coming soon)

Available from Pocket Books

---

christopher golden and rick hautala

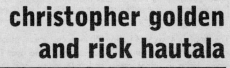

BURNING BONES

A *Body of Evidence*
thriller starring Jenna Blake

POCKET PULSE
New York London Toronto Sydney Singapore

An *Original* Publication of POCKET BOOKS

 POCKET PULSE published by
Pocket Books, a division of Simon & Schuster, Inc.
1230 Avenue of the Americas, New York, NY 10020

Copyright © 2001 by Christopher Golden

ISBN: 0-671-77584-7

First Pocket Pulse printing February 2001

10 9 8 7 6 5 4 3 2

POCKET PULSE and colophon are trademarks of Simon & Schuster, Inc.

Front cover illustration by Kamil Vojnar

Printed in the U.S.A.

for Barbra Isenberg
—C.G.

to Jesse, my son,
in hopes that your years at
"Somerset University" will not be as
dangerous, but certainly as interesting
—R.H.

acknowledgments

The authors would like to thank Lisa Clancy, Micol Ostow, Lori Perkins, Dr. Carlos Baleeiro (for a sickening conversation about burns), and their respective families.

BURNING BONES

prologue

If looks could kill.

That was the phrase that jumped into Laura Depuy's head when she saw Alan Nash hustling along the sidewalk toward her, twenty-seven minutes late by her watch. She glared daggers that would have dropped him in his tracks . . . if looks could kill. Laura liked Alan, she truly did. But she was a stickler for punctuality, and it frustrated her endlessly that he simply could not arrive anywhere less than fifteen minutes late. Fifteen. That was actually on time for Alan. It seemed like very little when she thought about it, but when twenty, thirty, or even forty minutes late was more common, it became a lot less tolerable.

To Laura, it represented a lack of respect and consideration. Alan did not understand how much she resented the implication that her time was somehow less valuable than his.

If looks could kill.

It was a Friday night, the first week of March, and though the days had started getting longer, and spring was tantalizingly close, it was still winter in New England. After dark there was never any mistake about that. It was cold. Laura shivered as she stood in front of DePasquale Brothers, a faded little Italian restaurant on a back street in Somerset, where she and Alan had dinner at least once every couple of months, mainly out of Alan's nostalgia. Laura didn't think much of the place, honestly. The decor was tacky, and the food was just okay, but Alan and his father had gone there all the time when he was a boy. Alan Sr. was dead now, so Laura was fairly good-natured about these regular visits to DePasquale's. It meant a lot to her boyfriend.

The one she wanted to kill at the moment.

She shivered as a party of seven parked across the street and hurried toward the front door of the restaurant, barely beating Alan there. They went in, only to be added to the list of those waiting to be seated inside. The place was not *that* good, but it was a neighborhood favorite, had been there forever, and on Friday nights, at least, it was busy.

Like tonight.

"Hey, babe. Sorry I'm late," Alan said quickly as he reached her. He slipped his arms around her and held her close, kissing her forehead.

Laura stood stiffly, unsmiling. Alan released her and stood back to regard her carefully.

"Come on, Laura. Don't be that way. I got held up at the office. I had a closing today, and it ran long."

"You *always* have a closing," she said bitterly. "And it *always* runs long."

"Look, the real estate market—"

"Is hot right now," she finished for him. "And who knows how long things will stay like this, and you're a real estate lawyer, and you've got to take advantage of the market while you can, and on and on."

He gazed at her sullenly. Several moments passed before he spoke again. "What do you want me to say?"

"I don't want you to say anything, Alan," she snapped. "I want you to do something. I want you to be *on time* for a change. Apparently that's too much to ask, but it's what I want."

Alan winced. "Don't you think you're overreacting just a little?"

Laura gaped at him, astounded at the depths of his tactlessness. She shuddered again, but now it was with anger rather than cold. A dozen responses came to mind, including two that would have ended their relationship on the spot. Despite her anger, that was not what she wanted. Alan was a decent, kind man, handsome and well-educated and funny when he wanted to be. He wore little round glasses that somehow matched his small mouth perfectly, and his hair was perpetually trimmed much too short, as if he believed being a lawyer required it. His absentmindedness could sometimes be charming. But the lateness, it was just so . . .

"Do you have any idea how rude you can be?" she sputtered, shaking her head. "I have been waiting here three quarters of an hour. You're half an hour late. Our reservation has long since been given away. Add to that the fact that it's cold out here, in case you hadn't noticed. Then throw in your general attitude, and that innocent, who-me facade of ignorance you work so hard to cultivate. Add that all up, Alan, with the fact that you do this all the time, and then tell me if you think I'm overreacting."

Eyes wide, Alan stared at her dumbfounded, then blinked a few times, as if someone had just popped an extra bright camera flash in front of his face.

"I thought you liked to eat here," he said, a tiny bit of whine in his voice.

"Oh, for God's sake, Alan!" Laura cried, throwing up her hands.

Alan laughed and reached for her. "No, no, I'm kidding. Really."

"Not funny," Laura told him firmly.

"I really am sorry," he said, his voice low. He reached out and grabbed her hands and held them gently. "You're right, of course. You always are. I'm an ass sometimes and I know it. And, yeah, sometimes I don't think about how annoying and inconvenient it is for you when I'm late. Mea culpa. Punish me as you see fit."

Laura looked at him, seething with anger.

"But I love you, Laura. I do, and all I can do is promise that I'll be more aware and more considerate. I swear I'll make it up to you. Starting right now. Want to go somewhere else? Capitol Grill? Il Bacio? You name it."

Though she still wanted to make him suffer, he was so earnest in his apology that Laura could not stop a tiny smile from tugging at the corners of her mouth. She rolled her eyes.

"Next time I will *not* wait. Are we clear on that? I will be gone."

"Clear as crystal. Waterford crystal."

With a sigh, she relented. "We can stay here. I know it's special to you. But I will take a rain check on *both* the Capitol Grill and Il Bacio, and I don't care how many closings you have, I want you to schedule a long weekend in April so we can go to New Orleans."

Alan grinned. "Done."

"Good," she said, and nodded once, sharply. "Now go in there and pull some strings and get us a table pronto, 'cause I'm starving."

He looked at her tenderly, then stepped close to kiss her lightly on the lips. "I love you, Laura."

"Hungry," she replied coolly. Then she smiled. "I love you, too."

Alan opened the door to DePasquale Brothers and stepped into the little foyer. A party of four was just leaving, and in the narrow space they had to jockey around one another. Alan bumped into one of the women, apologized, and then bumped a man as he backed up. He smiled sheepishly, and the expression only endeared him further to Laura.

She stood aside, holding the door open for the people who were leaving. Then she looked back into the foyer.

Alan was staring at her in alarm, as though he had just thought of something catastrophic. He spoke her name, but his voice had died and there was only a whisper left. For just a moment she feared he might be having a heart attack. There was panic in his eyes, and he stared at her as though he thought she might be able to do something to help him.

Then Alan burst into flame.

All at once, fire engulfed his body. His clothes and hair blazed even more brightly than the rest of him, but Laura could see that his skin was burning, too. Blistering. The flames covered him in shimmering waves.

Alan was screaming.

Laura realized that she was screaming too.

The people on the sidewalk and inside the restaurant were shouting in alarm and horror. A waiter thought quickly enough to run for the nearest fire extinguisher.

Alan fell to the ground and thrashed about, trying to put out the flames. His skin started to blacken, and after a moment, his thrashing slowed to convulsions.

By the time the waiter arrived and doused the flames with chemical foam, Alan was dead.

Laura kept screaming.

c h a p t e r   1

The world was gray, and Jenna Blake did not want to go to work.

The night before, Jenna's roommate, Yoshiko Kitsuta, had spent the night down the hall in Hunter LaChance's room. Even though the thought of boy-shy Yoshiko sleeping over at her boyfriend's would have been all but astonishing six months ago, Jenna did not find it all that remarkable now. On the one hand, she hoped that she had not done anything to make Yoshiko think Hunter could not sleep over in their room. But on the other hand, it was absolute bliss for her to have the room to herself on this cold, drizzly March Saturday morning.

Jenna snuggled under the covers and pretended even to herself that she was still asleep. It worked for a while. Icy raindrops pattered lightly against the window, which was open just a crack to let in the cold air. The combination of the chilly air and the scorched heat from the radiator, as well as the down comforter that covered her to the tip of her nose, was almost irresistible.

If only she could have stopped her mind from issuing pesky little thoughts, like the one about how she had promised Dr. Slikowski, her boss, that she would go in to work that day to catch up. He was the county medical examiner, operating out of Somerset Medical Center—which was conveniently attached to Somerset University, where Jenna went to school. She was a "diener," or pathology assistant, but had sort of become Robin to his Batman, in a way. Jenna liked that. It gave her purpose.

Today, however, she was feeling rather without purpose. Or wishing she was, at any rate. She had no greater ambition than to burrow deeper into her bed and watch cartoons. The thought of the autopsy transcriptions, filing, and other paperwork that awaited her was less than inspiring.

Still, eventually Jenna managed to climb out of bed. She wore thick socks and a knee-length nightshirt with angels on the front, and she shivered as the cold air from the window hit her. Reluctantly, she closed it, then put a pot of water on the hot plate to make herself cocoa. On TV, she surfed a few stations, scowled at the Three Stooges, and finally decided on a rerun of *Animaniacs* because she had loved the series so much as a kid.

It was after ten o'clock. Jenna had promised Dr. Slikowski, whom everyone called "Slick" behind his back, that she would be in at twelve-thirty. Briefly, she debated whether or not she should start reading *Twelfth Night*, which they would be discussing the following week in her Shakespeare class.

"That's not gonna happen," she said to herself, her voice still raspy from sleep.

With a smile, she fixed her cup of cocoa and sat down in front of the television set to chuckle along with the madcap antics of Wakko, Yakko, and Dot. When the show was over, Jenna reluctantly rose and went down the third-floor hallway to the girls' bathroom to shower. She left the television on, and it was company for her as she pulled on a dark green cotton turtleneck, a beige V-necked sweater, and blue jeans. Normally she would not have worn jeans to work, but it was the weekend, after all.

After she had dried her hair and put on eyeliner—the sum total of her makeup most days—Jenna glanced at the clock again and saw that it was not quite eleven-thirty. With a little time left to kill, she went to the small refrigerator and took out half a tuna fish sub she had ordered from Espresso's the night before. As she ate, she sat on the floor and read. It was an old book by Shirley Jackson called *We Have Always Lived in the Castle*, and it gave her the creeps. The overcast, damp day allowed the book to affect her even more deeply.

When it was time to leave for work, Jenna closed the book and slipped into her black leather jacket. As she left Sparrow Hall, heading across the residential quad, the whole campus seemed to have taken on a surreal quality, as if nothing was entirely there and tangible. It wasn't Somerset University, but the college's ghost that surrounded her.

You're losing it, Blake, she told herself, amused but also unnerved. Jenna was a constant reader. She tended to get carried off into the worlds she was reading about in novels, but the effect was not usually this dramatic. With a smile, she shook it off and walked across Carpenter Street to the Medical Center.

Jenna was surprised to see the lights on in the office as she walked down the hall, pulling her key card from her pocket. Slick had not said anything about coming in to work over the weekend, and neither had the pathology resident, Al Dyson, with whom Jenna had become quite friendly. It occurred to her that there might have been an autopsy that required immediate attention because of a police investigation. Though she would have enjoyed spending her afternoon alone, Jenna found that she was pleased by the idea of company now.

As she slipped her key card into the lock, she recognized the strains of jazz by Joshua Redman coming from inside the office and knew it must be Dr. Slikowski. Jazz was his refuge from the world.

The lock beeped, and she pushed into the office.

"Surprise!"

Jenna jumped and dropped her key card to the floor. Her eyes wide, she started laughing and shaking her head.

"My birthday isn't until tomorrow," she protested.

"A whole twenty-four hours away?" Dr. Slikowski asked. He rolled his wheelchair back and glanced at the others gathered around. "All right everyone, better pack it up. Come back tomorrow, about the same time."

"No, no, that's okay. Today's good," Jenna reassured him.

She was both stunned and heartened by the effort he had gone to. Dyson was there, of course, but so were Hunter and Yoshiko. Slick's girlfriend, Natalie Kerchak, leaned against the door to the M.E.'s inner office, sipping from a glass of punch. When Jenna caught her eye, Natalie smiled and offered a tiny wave. In the corner by Jenna's cubicle stood Danny Mariano and Audrey Gaines, Somerset police detectives Jenna and Slick had worked with many times, and with whom she had become friends.

"This is incredible," she told Slick. "Thank you."

"Happy birthday," he said in a low voice. "You make me feel old."

Dyson laughed. "That's because you *are* old, Walter, at least compared to her. What are you now, Jenna, twelve?"

"She's nineteen. And if she makes anyone feel old, it's me."

Stunned, Jenna turned to see her mother standing in the doorway behind her.

"Sorry I'm late," April Blake said. Then she shook her head and came toward her. "My little girl."

"Hey!" Jenna protested.

April rolled her eyes. "We're still having dinner

tonight, by the way. But when Walter told me about this, I couldn't resist."

Jenna gave her mother a hug, truly pleased to see her. But as she pulled away, she noticed her mother was watching her curiously.

"What?" she asked. "What's wrong?"

"Nothing. What could be wrong? Well, except that we're *both* getting older." April reached out to touch her daughter's face, chuckling to herself.

The odd look on her mother's face was gone, and Jenna wondered if it had been there at all, or if she had just imagined it. Dyson came over and gave her a hug, and she nudged him for not having spilled the beans about the party to her the day before. He only winked and then struck up a conversation with her mother. Slick was talking to Natalie, Danny, and Audrey across the room, and that left Jenna free to go over and give Hunter and Yoshiko big hugs.

"You *guys!*" she said. "I can't believe you didn't tell me about this."

"It's called a surprise for a reason, Jenna," Hunter reminded her.

"Besides," Yoshiko said, grinning, "we figured you could use some cheering up."

Jenna frowned. "What's that mean?" she asked. With a quick glance around, she studied the faces of her friends and coworkers and her mother. Nobody was looking at her.

"Nothing," Yoshiko said. "Just, y'know, after you broke up with Damon and everything else, you've been kind of . . . quiet. A little withdrawn. Dr. Dyson asked if they should do something for your birthday, and I thought it was a great idea."

Jenna wanted to argue. She was not the only one who had withdrawn. With the racial tensions that had erupted earlier in the semester on campus, things had not been easy for Yoshiko and Hunter any more than they had been for Jenna and her ex, Damon Harris. But Yoshiko and Hunter's relationship had survived.

"I'm fine. Really. I'm good, you guys. It's so sweet of Slick and Dyson to do this, and of everyone to come, but I hope it's just to celebrate my birthday, and not because everyone's thinking 'poor Jenna's got the blues' or something. 'Cause I'm good."

She shrugged.

Yoshiko gave her a doubtful look. "You sure?"

"Completely," Jenna told her. "And we're good." She glanced at Hunter, then reached out and poked him. "We're good, right?"

"We're better than good," he said, smiling widely.

Jenna returned the smile, then gave Yoshiko a quick hug. "Let's not get all weepy, though, okay? This is supposed to be a celebration of me, and I have a responsibility not to bring it down."

Her friends laughed, and Jenna was glad. She *did* have the blues, but she was working through them and planned to do that on her own. Though she loved them both, Hunter and Yoshiko had each other, and she did not feel as though either one of them would really be able to relate.

Smiling, Jenna excused herself to go speak to the others.

"Happy birthday, Jenna," Natalie said sweetly.

Jenna thanked her as the detectives echoed the woman's sentiments. Audrey eyed her for a moment.

"Hmm . . . you don't look any older," the detective said.

"I know, I'm still a kid, right?" Jenna replied, feigning exasperation.

"No," Audrey told her quite seriously. "I wouldn't say that at all."

Jenna beamed, but glanced away out of awkwardness. For whatever reason, Audrey's opinion mattered to Jenna. It meant a lot to know that this woman, who had previously defined her partially by her age, accepted her as an adult.

"Thanks."

Audrey offered a barely perceptible nod in return before joining in a conversation with Slick and Natalie. Jenna found herself suddenly alone with Danny Mariano. He was a ruggedly handsome, athletic guy with a tiny scar on his left eyebrow and dark blue eyes that looked purple in a certain light. Jenna was more than a little fond of Danny, but at thirty-two he was still a dozen years her senior and had made it abundantly clear that no matter how much he might care for her, there couldn't be anything more to it than that.

Which was okay, actually. Jenna might wish in her secret heart that things could be different, but Danny was a wonderful guy to know under any circumstances. And there was that old saying about being careful what you wish for.

14

"Happy birthday," he said softly.

To Jenna's surprise, he stepped in close and gave her a quick, little hug.

"People keep saying that," she replied. "I'm starting to get the idea that maybe this is a party, and nobody told me."

"There's cake," Danny revealed.

"Ah. Dead giveaway. Definitely a party."

He smiled sweetly and rubbed idly at the stubble on one cheek, and Jenna was tempted to tell him that he needed to shave. She didn't bother. It was very possible he and Audrey had been working all night and were on their way home to bed, rather than the opposite. Either way, she thought it was pretty cool that they had made the effort to come.

"Your mom seems nice," he told her.

"She is," Jenna agreed. "The best. Spoiled me rotten. Taught me how to be an independent woman."

Even as she said it, Jenna felt her smile falter. At the moment, the idea of being an independent woman still had a bit of a sting to it.

Danny frowned. "You okay?"

"There's another question people keep asking me." Jenna sighed, then met his concerned gaze. "I'm fine. Very. Do I have some kind of a sign on my forehead?"

Danny chuckled. "No. You just look like you're a million miles away. Like you're only half here and the other half is—"

"A million miles away?" Jenna suggested.

With a laugh, Danny shook his head. "That's just

what I was going to say. Seriously, though, if you ever want to talk, I'll always listen."

"You know what? I'd really like that," she replied. "I *am* fine, truly. But it would be nice to get off campus and clear my head."

"We're in the middle of a case, but how about lunch on Monday? Somewhere other than here. Your choice."

"I'm in."

They shared a silent moment before Slick rolled up beside Jenna in his wheelchair.

"Sorry to interrupt," he said, "but it's time to cut the cake. As Detective Mariano may have told you, we have work to do this afternoon."

Jenna glanced at Danny. "The case you're working on?" she asked.

Danny nodded.

"It's a grisly one," Slick warned.

Jenna sighed. "Aren't they always?"

The Somerset Police Department was housed in an aging brick municipal building just outside Kettle Square. Danny and Audrey had gone directly to the Medical Center from their homes that morning and so were in separate cars. When Danny pulled into the parking lot, Audrey was already hustling across the pavement toward the front door, trying to escape the cold drizzle that had been falling all morning. She had almost fully recovered from the stab wound in the chest she'd gotten recently in the line of duty, but he noticed that she still favored her left side.

The brick building was too familiar a sight, as far

as Danny was concerned. The burning death of Alan Nash the night before had kept them on the job until after one o'clock in the morning. Danny did not know about Audrey, but he had not fallen asleep until well after three. He hated being back here so soon. But they had to follow up on the Nash case before something got in the way.

He pulled his Buick into a space that was too narrow, and squeezed out, trying not to chip the paint on the car next to his. Then he jogged across the lot, annoyed by the rain. Inside, Danny shook off the water and the cold, and then started up the stairs to the detective squad room. When he entered, Audrey was already in conversation with Lieutenant Gonci. Nobody else was around.

"Morning, Danny," the older man said.

"Lieutenant."

"I was just telling Audrey that, at your suggestion, I sent Ross and Cardiff out to pick up the last of the witnesses from last night for questioning."

Danny glanced at Audrey. "The solo guy?"

Audrey nodded. "Yeah. Not that I've never had dinner alone, but he was a ways away from home to be there by himself."

The lieutenant studied her. "His statement from the scene seemed a little jumbled. See if he can give us a better idea of the circumstances. We've got a mystery here. Maybe it's not homicide, but it's ugly as hell and I need to make sense of it."

Danny frowned. "I hope we can. I'm not thrilled with the idea of spontaneous combustion."

"Neither am I," Gonci said grumpily. "While we are not officially ruling out the possibility, the Somerset Police Department is dubious as to the existence of spontaneous human combustion. That's right from the chief. What about your other witnesses? Anything there?"

"Three of them were dining together, no connection to Nash as far as we can tell. We're looking hard at the girlfriend, though. Maître d' said he saw them having an argument out front right before it happened. On the other hand, unless she was able to douse him in gasoline and set him alight without anyone noticing, I don't know how she could have done it."

Before anyone could reply, Ross and Cardiff, accompanied by Victor Frost, came into the squad room, shaking off their raincoats. The detectives were part of the old-boy network, though only Cardiff was actually old enough to qualify. He was fiftysomething, rumpled and a little overweight, and he had been smoking more since a layer of kevlar had kept a bullet from taking his life five or six weeks earlier. His partner was thinner, younger, but just as grumpy.

In comparison, Frost, the witness, looked like a shiny new penny. Despite the rain outside, he wore a stylish brown leather coat, dark, crisp blue jeans, and white Reebok sneakers, all of which looked brand new. His short blond hair was perfectly combed, as if he had somehow managed to walk between raindrops, and his square eyeglasses screamed hipness a little too loudly.

"Our friend," Danny muttered to Audrey. "Like a brand-new toy just out of the package. It's a little creepy."

While Ross guided the witness to the interview room, Cardiff sidled over to them, putting on his best curmudgeon face. He shot Lieutenant Gonci a reluctantly respectful look, then turned to the others.

"You got any more errands you need run, Mariano? Gaines? Anything? 'Cause, y'know, me and Dwight, we got nothing better to do today than your legwork."

With a quizzical expression, Danny glanced at Audrey, who met his gaze. Almost in unison, they shrugged.

"No, Mike. We're good," Danny told him.

"But thanks for asking," Audrey added, with as much sincerity as she could muster.

The gruff old cop muttered angrily under his breath and walked away. When Danny turned to Lieutenant Gonci, he thought he caught the ghost of a smile on his superior's face, but then it was gone.

"You want to observe, Lieutenant?"

Gonci shook his head. "You two go ahead. Give me your impressions when you're through."

Audrey sat across the table from Frost in the interview room. She leaned forward, scrutinizing him, but the guy just sat there as though at any second he might yawn and start to clean his nails.

"Is this going to take long?" Frost asked, sounding bored.

Danny didn't blame him. The whole process was boring. The three other witnesses had been together as a group at the restaurant when Alan Nash had burned. A guy named Bart Randeau; his wife, Anne; and her sister, Lizabeth Orton. They had been there celebrating Mr. Randeau's birthday.

"Not too long," Danny told him. On a whim, he asked Frost if he knew the Randeaus or Lizabeth Orton.

"I thought the dead guy was named Ash," Frost replied with a frown. "Last night, when I gave a statement, I thought—"

"The deceased was Alan Nash. That's right. Did you know him?" Audrey prodded.

"No. Who's this Randeau, then?"

"You don't know any of those people?" Danny studied him.

Frost shrugged. "Nope. What else do you want to know?"

"What I'd like to know, Victor, is why you were at that restaurant last night," Danny said.

Another shrug. "Guy can't have dinner alone?"

"But you didn't order dinner, did you?" Audrey asked. "You were at the bar."

"I had a long workday yesterday," Frost told her. "I thought I'd relax. Have a drink. Wind down before I ate."

Audrey leaned back a little in her chair, drawing the man's attention. "The bartender remembered you pretty well, Mr. Frost. She says you were there for more than an hour. That you drank only ginger ale."

"All right, you caught me," Frost replied. He shrugged. "I thought I might meet someone in the bar. It's been known to happen."

Danny shook his head in disbelief. "Okay, wait, let me see if I'm following you. I'm not all that bright, y'know? You live in Cambridge, where there are hundreds of nice restaurants and bars where single people go to meet each other. But to try to make a meaningful romantic connection, you go to the next city over to a run-down Italian restaurant with a tiny bar playing Frank Sinatra while the Celtics game is on the TV?"

The man stopped fidgeting and shot a hard look at Danny. For a moment, he was very focused. "Are you mocking me, Detective Mariano? Because if you are—"

"No, not at all. Just trying to understand something that I'm apparently not smart enough to grasp."

"Apparently," Frost replied coldly. "I don't want to be with the kind of woman I could meet at one of those meat markets you're talking about. I always feel like I'll have a better chance of finding an interesting person who isn't already on the hunt by going to out-of-the-way places. Twisted logic it may be, but it's all mine."

Audrey tapped a pen on the table and Frost stared at it.

"Had you ever been to that particular restaurant before?" she asked.

The man frowned. "No." He crossed his arms and sighed.

"And you never had occasion to meet the deceased, Alan Nash?" Audrey asked.

"For the third time, no. Never met him. Never knew him. Never saw him before. Now may I leave? I feel bad the guy's dead. It was a pretty horrible thing. I agreed to come down here because I figured it was the right thing to do, tell you what I saw. Which was basically nothing. One minute he's with his date or whatever, the next he's the human torch."

"I guess it's just your bad luck that you happened to be there when the guy spontaneously combusted and burned to death," Danny said archly.

"You can say that again," Frost mumbled. "May I go?"

Danny and Audrey exchanged a look, and a silent communication passed between them, honed over the years that they had been partners. Audrey's expression told Danny that she had nothing else. Danny tilted his head slightly to one side and raised one eyebrow. *Your call,* he was telling her.

"Yeah, you can go. We may want to ask some more questions later," Audrey told him.

Frost grumbled. "Color me stunned," he said.

Danny and Audrey watched him as he slipped his coat on and went toward the door.

"What do you think?" he asked Audrey when Frost had gone.

"He's a creep," Audrey replied.

Danny smiled. "Yeah, but what do you think?"

"He didn't see anything that'll help us. Eccentric, yeah, but he doesn't seem any more connected than the Randeaus to the victim. We should do a background check on all of them just to be thorough, but I'm thinking if Nash's death wasn't some kind of bizarre phenomenon—if we find out there's some explanation to the burning that indicates somebody did it to him—it'll be the girlfriend. Nothing else makes sense."

"Nothing about this makes sense," Danny replied.

The smell of charred flesh was the worst part.

Jenna had gotten used to the stench of formaldehyde. In her time working as a diener for Slick, she had seen the grisliest of murder and accident victims, had removed and dissected organs, and had even sutured closed the massive incision required for an autopsy. As such, though she felt absolute revulsion at the state of Alan Nash's corpse and though she recoiled when Dr. Slikowski cut into the charred remains and there was a crackling sound from the burned skin, Jenna was all right. She had learned to distance herself from such things. But the smell.

"Oh God," Jenna whispered, cupping a gloved hand over the mask that covered her face.

Beside her, Dyson nodded. "The odor's awful. But the fan is up as high as it goes."

"I'll be all right," Jenna told him. She was determined not to let it get to her, but her legs felt like they almost buckled.

Slick expertly navigated his wheelchair around the autopsy table, as usual. Narrating the autopsy into the tape recorder that was always present, he pulled back to give Dyson room to use the bone saw to remove a portion of the ribs and sternum. Then Slick returned to the table. He worked the controls that lowered it to give him better access and began to examine the cadaver's newly exposed organs.

The medical examiner frowned.

"Al, show me the section of bone we just removed," he said.

Dyson lifted the rib cage and displayed it for Slick. Over the top of his mask, Jenna saw the M.E.'s eyes widen behind his glasses.

"What is it?" she asked.

Slick glanced at her. She knew he did not like to offer any opinion at all until the autopsy was completed, until all the data had been collected.

This time was no different.

Slick didn't reply, and they went about the process as usual. Jenna, to her own horror, grew used to the acrid stench of burned flesh. She noticed that Slick took several samples of the dead man's burned skin and of the muscle layer directly beneath.

When they were through and Dyson was wheeling the body back to the morgue, Slick pulled off his mask and gloves. Jenna removed hers as well and then hung both of their lab coats in a locker.

Impatiently, she turned to him. "Well?"

He smiled. "Wait for Dr. Dyson. He should hear this, too."

"Then let's wait in the hall. It still stinks in here,"

Jenna told him, waving her hand in front of her face.

They went out together and waited outside the door to the morgue. A few minutes later Dyson emerged. He seemed startled to find the two of them looking at him so intensely.

"I take it you have a theory?" he asked, studying Slick's expression.

Slick nodded. "So much for spontaneous combustion."

"I didn't think you believed in it anyway," Dyson replied.

"Neither did I," Jenna added.

"I've never seen a case," the M.E. explained. "But given the apparently legitimate sources of a number of reports, I'm willing to keep an open mind on the subject. On the other hand, all reported cases that I found in my research earlier this morning indicate that the source of the fire is internal. The bodies of the supposed victims were burned worse inside than out, or burned relatively uniformly."

"And that isn't the case here," Jenna said, understanding at last. "The muscles were barely touched by the flames, and even the skin was only badly charred on the outside."

"True. In fact, Mr. Nash died of cardiac failure. Likely brought on by the trauma of being burned."

"But wait a minute," Dyson put in, frowning. "If the burns were all external . . ."

"Then the source of the fire was external. Which

means it was either a freak accident of some kind, or else a murder," Slick finished.

"But there were witnesses. There was no source for the flame. It just . . . happened," Jenna protested. "How can that be?"

Slick smiled. "That's the question of the day, isn't it?"

c h a p t e r 2

The soft, orange glow of candlelight filled the restaurant. Jenna glanced around at the patrons seated around the main dining room in Samuel's. For such a large room, each table seemed surprisingly private, yet Jenna could not help staring at the clientele, the men in three-piece suits and tuxedos, and the women wearing gorgeous dresses and gowns highlighted with dazzling jewelry. It was foolish to feel this way, she knew, but even as dressed up as she was, she felt a little bit out of place. No doubt it was just her mood lately, but she was not going to let that or anything else ruin her evening out with her mother.

"You didn't have to take me to a place so expensive," Jenna whispered, leaning forward with her hands folded on the crisply starched tablecloth.

Her mother was a surgeon and Jenna was an only child. Her father had left when she was very young, so the two of them had essentially been a dynamic duo all of her life. When April Blake had vacation time she tended to overdo it, and as a result Jenna had traveled with her mother to a lot of places that most of the kids at Natick High had never seen. How many kids her age had been to Istanbul? Not a lot.

April also had a history of overdoing it for Jenna's birthday. That meant expensive dinners and even more expensive dresses.

"It isn't every day your daughter turns nineteen, and it's been far too long since we've come here," Dr. April Blake replied with a beaming smile.

"I think it was my sixteenth birthday," Jenna said. "You spoil me."

"That's true," her mother teased. "But I can't help myself. I just can't believe how proud I am of you." April savored the taste of the wine for a moment, then carefully placed her glass on the table and sat back in her chair, idly running her hand over the tablecloth, smoothing it.

Jenna cringed a little inside and smiled as she glanced down at her folded hands. She knew her mother had more serious subjects in mind.

They sat in silence for a few moments; then her mother cleared her throat to draw Jenna's attention.

"So tell me, really, how are you doing, honey?" she asked, leaning forward and peering intently at Jenna. The light caught her eyes just right and made them glisten like rain-washed stone.

"I'm doing fine . . . really, I am. Couldn't be better."

The lie left a bitter taste in Jenna's mouth, and she

had no doubt that her mother saw right through it. The only question was, how hard was she going to push to get the truth?

"I just know that sometimes breakups can be pretty tough," her mother said. She tilted her head back and, looking up at the ceiling, took a deep breath. "Your father and I used to come here a lot, you know. Before you were born. And it's where my lawyer took me to *celebrate* after the divorce was final."

Jenna squared her shoulders, determined not to let herself get drawn out. If she did, the next thing she knew her mother would be asking her if maybe she shouldn't come home for a while to take a break from everything . . . as if running home every time something went wrong was the solution to life's problems.

"So maybe . . . I don't know," her mother said, sounding almost wistful, "maybe I picked this place because this is where we go when we've had our hearts broken."

"Mom, come on," Jenna said. "Okay, I'll admit that I—that it hurt, all right? But life goes on. I'm doing okay. Really. I love school, and my job is going great. Better than great. You don't have to worry about me. Honest."

"I know I don't," her mother said, her voice catching slightly, "but I still do. I'm your mother. It comes with the territory. When you have children of your own, you'll find out what it's like."

"I probably will, but hopefully that's a long way in

the future," Jenna said with a light laugh. "I can see that it wasn't right for Damon and me. I really can. It would never have worked out in the end."

April opened her mouth and seemed about to say something, but then caught herself and, smiling weakly, sat back in her chair.

"And even if it could have worked out," Jenna continued, keeping her voice low so she would not disturb the other customers. "Even if I had wanted it to work, it was up to *me* to do it. I'm nineteen, remember—"

"How could I forget?" her mother said as she took another little swallow of wine.

"Well, it's true," Jenna persisted. "I'm nineteen years old. I have to make my own decisions and live with them. And so far, all in all, I think I've done a pretty good job of it."

"I think you have, too, sweetheart," her mother said earnestly, "but I also don't want you to forget that, no matter *how* old you are, no matter *what* the problem is, you can always talk to me. Always! We were 'just us girls' for so long, and I know there's more to your life than that now. But when you need it to be, it can always be 'just us girls' again, even just for a little while. You realize that, don't you? That I'll always be there for you?"

"Don't be silly. Of course I do," Jenna said.

Her voice was husky with emotion as she reached across the table and clasped her mother's hand, giving it a tight squeeze. The moment was broken when their waiter appeared. He was a tall, young man with dark, wavy hair and pale blue eyes, not much older than she was, Jenna thought. Kind of cute, too.

Maybe I really will be okay, Jenna thought.

Danny was wearing street clothes and his hair was still damp from the shower when he walked out into the hallway from the locker room. He was just turning down the hallway, heading for his office to get his jacket, when Audrey called out to him from the squad break room.

He turned and saw her sitting at a table, talking with two other cops, Bellamy and Collins.

"Just got a call from Slick," Audrey said.

Danny tensed, dreading that she might tell him that the M.E. had called to say that he needed to see them right away. He had a date with Kim and was already running late. They had gone out for a few months the previous year but she had grown too frustrated with the hectic life of a cop—or just this cop; Danny was never quite sure. But when she called to give it one last shot, he had jumped at the chance. Kim was a kind, intelligent woman, and pretty patient under normal circumstances. But this was the first time he had been able to schedule a get-together with her after she called. If he was late this time— well, he didn't even want to think about it because he *wasn't* going to be late.

"And?" Danny asked.

"And," Audrey said, "he's determined that there's

no way this could have been a case of spontaneous human combustion."

"Okay," Danny said with a small shrug, barely registering what Audrey was saying.

"If it had been SHC," Audrey continued, "the victim would have been burned more on the inside than the outside. That's how cases like that go, as if the heat comes from an internal source. But our guy was burned worse on the outside, so no matter how much—"

Danny sighed. "Are you saying we have a murder investigation?"

"Yeah. It looks that way, partner," Audrey said with a curt nod.

An hour later Danny and Kim were seated at the bar in Panda Garden, waiting for a table. Kim looked great, there was no doubt about that. Her long black hair glistened like satin in the dim light of the restaurant. She had just gotten back from a week in Florida, and her face had a tanned, healthy glow. But throughout the drive over to the restaurant, and even after they had ordered drinks, Danny could not stop thinking about what Audrey had told him just before he left. He was not sure if he believed in spontaneous human combustion, and he knew Audrey thought it was a myth. Now—thankfully—it wasn't an issue.

But if it wasn't spontaneous combustion, then what was it? he wondered. *We'll have to look at the possibility of some kind of freak accident, but what are the chances of that? Looks like someone set Alan Nash on fire. But if so, the mystery just got deeper. The girlfriend? Someone else?*

Why someone would want to do that was a big question. The biggest one, though, was *how?*

"You want to know the problem with us?" Kim asked, breaking the silence that had settled between them.

Pulled from his musings, Danny stopped twirling the little paper umbrella that had come with his Hawaiian Sunset and looked up at her, his eyebrows raised questioningly.

"The problem is," Kim continued, her voice low and steady, "that whenever we go out to eat, whenever we do anything together, there's always three of us."

Danny frowned and shook his head, trying to focus his attention fully on her.

"What do you mean?" he asked; but even as he was saying it, he knew exactly what she meant. Right now, even though no one could see him, there was a third person sitting between them at the bar. His name was "The Job."

"What I mean is, ever since you got here, you've hardly said *boo*. The sad thing is, I know it isn't *me*. It would be easier if you just didn't like me or if you were a total jerk or something. But I can tell by the expression on your face that you're mulling over something that happened at work today, a case or something."

Danny could see the hurt in her eyes, and he

wanted to tell her that it wasn't so, that all he was thinking about was how great she looked and how much he liked being with her. But *he* knew, and he knew that *she* knew it would be a lie. He could never stop thinking about work. If it wasn't the Alan Nash case, it would have been something else. It was the way he was built, part of the wiring.

"Look, Danny," Kim said. She leaned toward him and took one of his hands into both of hers. She smiled thinly as she gave his hand a tight squeeze. "You're a terrific guy. You really are. And I'm sure that someday you'll meet a woman who'll be able to get through to you, or else she'll be able to put up with your preoccupation with your work."

"No, Kim. It's not that—"

"Let me finish, all right?" Kim said, her voice showing just a touch of steel. "I like you . . . I like you a lot. I was feeling badly about the way things ended before and thought I should give you another chance. Now I know that was a mistake. We both know that it's just not going to work out for us."

"Maybe we haven't tried hard enough," Danny said. "Maybe *I* haven't."

"I don't know if you're capable of it," Kim said softly. "I don't want to hurt you, Danny, but I also don't want to get hurt myself. I'm not going to be in a relationship where I come in second."

Danny started to protest, but she hushed him with a wave of her hand.

"I'm really sorry," she said as she stood and took her coat from the back of the chair. Danny got up and made a move to help her put it on, but she turned away from him so he couldn't.

"Wait a minute," Danny said.

With one last sad shake of her head, Kim strode out of the bar.

He almost ran after her, but he knew that it would be a waste of time. Cringing under the curious stares of the handful of customers who had seen what had happened, and feeling absolutely deflated and alone, Danny sat back down. Resting his hand on the edge of the bar, he picked up the little paper umbrella and began twirling it between his thumb and forefinger.

Perhaps the saddest thing about the entire incident, he thought, *is that not thirty seconds later I realize that I've stopped thinking about Kim. I'm thinking about the Alan Nash case, and what Audrey and I are going to do about it next.*

She's right, he thought. But he felt helpless to do anything about that.

"Oh, hey, guys. I didn't expect to see you here."

Jenna closed the door and shrugged off her coat. Yoshiko and Hunter were sitting on the floor, their backs against the side of the lower bunk propped up with pillows. Yoshiko had one arm around Hunter's waist and was leaning her head against his shoulder. She had a faraway look in her eyes as she glanced up at Jenna. The TV was on with the sound turned down low. Jenna's first and only impression was that—even though this was just as much her room as Yoshiko's—she was intruding.

"The new Jackie Chan movie just came out on video," Hunter said with almost childish excitement in his voice. He shifted to one side and patted the floor beside him. "We just started it. Come on. Have a seat."

Jenna considered his offer, but only for a moment. She was not a huge Jackie Chan fan, but his movies did make her laugh, and right now, for some reason, she felt like she could use a good laugh.

Still . . .

"Thanks, but no," she finally said as she hung up her coat in the closet. "I, ah, I've got some reading to do."

She couldn't help but feel as though both her roomie and Hunter were—well, not really angry about her showing up, but maybe just a little put out.

"How was dinner with your mom?" Yoshiko asked. "Where did you go?"

"Oh, it was incredible," Jenna replied brightly. "We went to Samuel's over on Tremont Street. Have either of you ever been there?"

Yoshiko and Hunter glanced at each other, then shook their heads.

"We'll all have to go there sometime," Jenna offered, "to celebrate something really special."

"Sounds good to me," Hunter said, but he seemed a bit distracted, his attention focused more on the TV now that the previews were over, and the movie had started.

"Well," Jenna said, "I have to get started reading *Twelfth Night*."

Her copy of *Twelfth Night* was over on her desk,

but she felt suddenly self-conscious, walking between them and the TV to get it. "Maybe I'll go downstairs to the lounge and read there," she said as she skittered in front of them and quickly scooped the book off her desk.

"We can leave, if you'd like," Yoshiko offered. Without waiting for Jenna to reply, she shifted her feet under her and started to stand. "Hunter has a VCR in his room. We can watch it down there."

Looking a little dazed, as if he was not quite sure what was going on, Hunter glanced away from the tube.

"Oh, yeah . . . sure," he said good-naturedly. Leaning forward, he popped the tape out.

"No. Come on, you guys," Jenna said, feeling suddenly foolish, like a spoiled child who had insisted on getting her way and then felt guilty because she got it. "You were all settled in."

"You'll never be able to concentrate downstairs," Yoshiko said, "especially if Steve and his friends are playing Hearts, which they always are." She was on her feet now and moving toward the door. Hunter was a step or two behind her, the tape clutched in his hand.

"You're sure you don't mind?" Jenna said.

Yoshiko pursed her lips and shook her head. "This is your room, too, and if you want to study here, we'll find someplace else to play. It's no problem."

Jenna could not tell if the tension she felt was real or imagined, if Yoshiko was really being sweet and courteous or was angry with her, but she was tired of playing the game of trying to "outnice" each other, so she finally relented.

"Okay. Thanks. I really appreciate it."

With that, Hunter and Yoshiko left. Once she was alone in the room, Jenna heaved a deep sigh and sat down on her bed. It made her sad to think that she was having such awkward feelings about her best friends, but she did not know how to address those feelings, how to put them into words. After adjusting the reading light on her desk and propping herself up with her pillow, she sat back and opened the play to the first page.

" 'If music be the food of love, play on,' " she read out loud.

Marking her place with her finger, she closed the book and stared blankly at the door.

"Did I just miss something back there?" Hunter asked as he and Yoshiko walked hand in hand down the corridor toward his room.

"I—I'm not sure," Yoshiko replied softly.

Her stomach felt all knotted up, and she realized that she needed to take a deep breath. Stopping in the middle of the hallway, she turned to Hunter and stared deeply into his eyes. He smiled back at her, and she could feel the warm pressure of his hand holding hers, but something didn't feel right.

"I just . . . with Jenna," Yoshiko said, shaking her head.

"Umm . . . I know," Hunter said, nodding sadly.

"She's hurting right now, and we've got to do what we can to help her out."

Yoshiko started to say what was on her mind but caught herself. Closing her eyes, she took another deep breath as she carefully considered how to say what she wanted to say.

"You know, that's just it," she finally muttered. "We *have* been trying really hard to help her. Both of us have been totally patient and understanding."

"Well, I just know that I'll never forget how much of a support she was when my sister died," Hunter said, a slight catch in his voice.

"I know," she said, "but with Jenna I . . . it's like every time I reach out to her, there's this . . . this wall between us that I just can't break through."

"She's got a lot to deal with," Hunter said. "She took it pretty hard when she found out about Damon and Caitlin."

"Okay, but it's not the end of the world," Yoshiko said. "And what does that have to do with us, the three of us, I mean?"

She did not like the flash of anger she was feeling, but now that she had started to unload, she wasn't going to stop.

"She mopes around all the time, feeling sorry for herself, like she's the first person in the world to have her heart broken. I guess I just feel useless because I want to help her, and instead I end up getting frustrated with her."

Hunter smiled at Yoshiko, obviously at a loss for words until, finally, he cleared his throat. "She's our friend, and I think, no matter what, we have to hang in there with her until she gets through this."

"I know. I know," Yoshiko replied, looking down at the floor as she shook her head. "It's just that . . . I don't know what to say. She's so distant, and yet it feels like she doesn't even think anything's wrong."

Sparrow Hall straddled the imaginary line that separated the residential quad from the academic quad. Both were sprawls of grass and paths and trees surrounded by buildings, the one bordered by dormitories and the other flanked by faculty offices and classrooms. Most of the structures were old and grand, though some of the dorms built later did not have the aesthetic value of the academic buildings. Fletcher Avenue separated the two quads, just as—on the other side of the residential quad—Carpenter Street separated the main campus from the medical school and Somerset Medical Center.

Jenna cut across the residential quad on Sunday morning and marveled at the number of people moving about this early who did not look like the walking dead. Okay, sure, it was bright and sunny and even, God forbid, warm for March, but it was still a Sunday morning at not quite eight, and it was just *wrong* for so many notoriously sluggish college students to be so energetic. There were joggers and walkers and bicyclists and a group sitting in front of Hyde Hall talking animatedly. Most of them even looked as though they had already showered. A guy in a sweat-shirt and shorts—shorts in March!—sat on a concrete wall, leaning against the dorm as he read from a paperback.

It was an entirely different species of human, Jenna figured. Early birds. As she walked past Hyde Hall on a beeline for Keates, she felt self-conscious in her sweats, with her auburn hair tied back into a sloppy ponytail. She tried to be inconspicuous and happily succeeded.

Breakfast that morning had consisted of orange juice and apple cinnamon Pop Tarts in her dorm room as she read through *Twelfth Night* for Shakespeare class. At first Jenna had had difficulty getting into Shakespeare, but now that she understood the rhythms, it really was won-derful writing.

Jenna jogged up the front steps of Keates Hall. With all the healthy exercise types around, she thought she might feel less self-conscious if she had the same spring in her step that they all seemed to have. It helped, but only a little. As a general rule she only came to Keates to eat in the basement dining hall, but the building was also one of the larger dor-mitories in the uphill section of the campus.

Her friend Roseanne Kerner lived on the second floor. Jenna did not bother jogging up the stairs. After their Medical Anthropology class the previous Thursday afternoon, Roseanne had somehow managed to get Jenna to agree to meet her for a walk this morning. The long, fast, exercise kind. Jenna normally liked to exercise, but ever since she started attending Somerset, she had fallen into a pattern of classes and work and sleeping as late as humanly possible that did not allow for much in the way of healthy physical activity. Roseanne was on a mission to change all that. She *preached* exercise. But not in an annoying way, just in a manner that made Jenna feel vaguely guilty and sort of embarrassed.

Roseanne had even threatened to get Jenna into a regular regimen. It might have caused Jenna to shudder to think about such a thing, but actually, she was secretly pleased by the idea. She needed a change, she knew that. Maybe adding this sort of routine—not to mention getting closer to Roseanne, making a new friend—would be exactly what she needed.

At the door to room 221, Jenna knocked.

Roseanne opened the door instantly, a broad smile on her face. Cold air blew out of the room and Jenna saw that both windows were open at least four or five inches. The other girl was dressed in more proper exercise clothes than the baggy Somerset University sweats Jenna wore. Roseanne's outfit looked more like she was about to teach a kick boxing or aerobics class than anything else. She wore a Boston Red Sox cap and had a fanny pack strapped around her waist, and she was practically bouncing on the balls of her feet with energy.

"I hate you," Jenna drawled.

With a laugh, Roseanne stepped out into the hallway and locked the door behind her. "You're going to be fine, Jenna. Trust me."

"It's nice out today, Rosie, but not that nice. Do you like it cold?"

"Just airing the place out," Roseanne told her. "I like that spring smell. It's the reason I couldn't live anywhere but New England. Plus in the morning it's so peaceful, y'know?"

"No," Jenna retorted. "This is a time of day I usually only see through slitted eyes."

Then she laughed. It was impossible not to, given Roseanne's infectious enthusiasm. Jenna had taken to the girl almost immediately when they had first met in Medical Anthro. She was from a wealthy town not far from Natick, where Jenna had grown up. Roseanne was direct, and so positively charged that in her presence it was impossible not to feel lifted up by her. She was an unassuming girl who wore no makeup on her cute, pixie face, thin nose and bright blue, sparkling eyes. She had a straight blond bob that fell to her shoulders and she stood no more than five feet tall, probably less. Roseanne was a freshman, but she looked like she might still be in junior high. It was just another reason she was so disarming.

Thoughts of age reminded Jenna that today was her birthday. It was a fact she was glad Roseanne did not know. They were friends, but not so close Jenna had made a big deal of her upcoming birthday. She just wanted to have a nice day and get to know her friend better.

Roseanne was the type who seemed to automatically take charge of any situation and yet never seemed to step on any toes or aggravate anyone by doing so. It was a personality trait that reminded Jenna greatly of another friend, Hunter's sister, Melody LaChance, who had been killed during the first semester. It was bittersweet to be reminded of Melody, but Jenna was glad of it. She had no desire to forget her friend. And she thought it said an awful lot about Roseanne that she could sometimes remind Jenna of Melody.

"You look very sexy, by the way," Roseanne told her, eyeing her baggy sweats as they went down the stairs to the foyer of Keates Hall.

"Hey!" Jenna protested. "Put away the sarcasm. It's too early in the morning. You said get some exercise, do some walking. There was nothing in there about looking good. And I remind you . . . it *is* eight o'clock in the morning."

"Just saying I think the guys will be disappointed," Roseanne said airily.

"Guys?" Jenna snapped. "What guys? We're walking here, not going to a party."

They began to walk—much too fast for Jenna's liking but she knew she had to keep up—across the quad to Fletcher and then downhill.

"There are lots of very athletic guys around campus this time of the morning. Especially on weekends," Roseanne explained. "You just have to know where to look."

Jenna groaned and glanced around at the guys on

bikes and those running. Muscular, healthy guys, some of whom were very good-looking. "I am not out here to be looked at by guys. I've had enough of guys lately."

"They look. Nothing you can do about it. As far as whether you've had enough, I never met your last boyfriend, but I'm thinking maybe what you need is a little flirtation to shake your head out of the clouds and get you back down here to the real world, where life continues on without you."

Jenna was about to protest but Roseanne's last words echoed in her head. *Life continues on without me,* she thought. *Damon derailed me.* She did not necessarily agree with Roseanne about the flirtation thing, but the girl's words and her overall attitude were certainly having an effect.

"Maybe you're right," Jenna conceded.

"Maybe?" Roseanne asked, aghast. "Listen, chicky, you're gonna have to learn that Rosie's always right. Count on it."

Her tone indicated that Roseanne was perfectly aware of the absurdity of that statement. Jenna gave her a doubtful glance and they both started giggling. It felt good to be silly. Jenna had almost forgotten what *silly* was all about.

As they were speed walking across Sterling Lane, a darkly handsome guy with a muscular build and wide eyes jogged toward them. He smiled as he went past.

"Morning," he said breathlessly.

"Morning," the girls replied in unison.

"He was checking you out," Roseanne said, glancing over her shoulder at the receding jogger. "Hmm nice butt, too."

"Come on. He just said *good morning*. Besides, how do you know he wasn't checking *you* out?"

"He was *so* checking you out," Roseanne said. She sighed. "So much for my outfit. Maybe I should get a set of rumpled, gray, shapeless sweats."

Jenna whacked her on the arm and they started laughing again. Even with the sun warming the air up, the breeze still carried a bit of a chill. They walked down to the football field where the Somerset Colts played and did laps around the ten-lane track that circled the field. There were a lot of people exercising down there, and Roseanne was right that many of them were male. They laughed a lot that morning. When they were done, Jenna found herself agreeing to walk again soon.

Yoshiko was reading *The Birds* by Aristophanes for her Greek and Roman comedy class when she heard Jenna's key slip into the lock. Sting was on the CD player, and she had pillows stacked up against the brick wall, snuggled into her top bunk, content and peaceful. When she realized that her roommate had returned, all that instantly changed, and Yoshiko hated the way it felt. It made her sad to realize that she was not at all happy that Jenna had returned.

The door swung open, and her roommate stood there with red cheeks, looking tired but with a little smile on her face. When she caught sight of Yoshiko up on the top bunk, she faltered. Yoshiko realized that it must have been the expression on her face that put Jenna off and she felt even worse.

"Hey," Jenna said.

"Hey. Where've you been?"

"Getting a little exercise," Jenna replied as she closed the door behind her and started to kick off her sneakers. "Surprisingly, the world didn't end."

Yoshiko did not know how to respond to that. Jenna was kidding with her. But the shadow of the way things had been still hung between them. Jenna pulled off her sweatshirt and mopped her neck and belly with it. She continued to get undressed and then pulled her robe on.

"I feel really gritty. I'm going to go take a shower. Sorry if I interrupted your work."

When Jenna's hand touched the doorknob, Yoshiko could not stand it anymore. "Jenna."

As if she were deflating, Jenna's shoulders slumped and she turned to face Yoshiko. Her expression was pained, her features pinched, a reverse image of the smiling girl who had come into the room minutes before.

"I've been such a bitch," Jenna rasped.

"No, Jenna, it's—"

"Yoshiko."

"True. You have been."

"I'm sorry." Jenna sighed. "I've just been trying to deal. To make it all go away. And you guys seemed so happy that I guess . . . at first I thought I just didn't want to bother you with my problems, but maybe it was also that I'm just a bit jealous. Not like I wanted you and Hunter to break up, but . . . I've got this four-year-old inside me, whining *why-me-and-not-them*, y'know?"

Yoshiko slipped off her bunk and stood facing her roommate. "I know," she said. It bothered her to see Jenna—who was usually so together—so obviously unraveled. "I've been pretty mad at you, too. Not just 'cause of how you've been acting, but because you weren't letting us help. We're your friends, J. Or have you forgotten that part?"

"No, I . . . maybe I did."

Yoshiko smiled at her and shifted on her feet, a bit uneasy. It was only now that they were finally talking about it that she realized how much she had been hurt by Jenna's unwillingness to confide in her, to come to her for help.

"Do you forgive me?" Jenna asked.

"Yeah," Yoshiko replied. "As long as you forgive us. I guess we could've pushed a little harder."

"Maybe. And maybe I just would've retreated further. I can be pretty stubborn, y'know?"

"Really? I can't imagine," Yoshiko said with a laugh. "When would I have ever gotten that impression? Listen, we can't go tonight 'cause I have too much homework to catch up on, but can we go out in the next couple of nights, just the three of us? Get away from here, someplace that's not on this campus?"

"I'd love it," Jenna replied.

She hesitated a moment, then threw her arms around Yoshiko. The two girls hugged each other tightly. Yoshiko felt the final bits of the barrier that had separated them in recent weeks breaking away. At length Jenna let her go and then went back to the door, still apparently planning to go down the hall to take a shower.

At the door she turned back again. "We're good?" Jenna asked.

Yoshiko grinned. "Better than good."

Jenna was still buzzing on Monday from the realizations she had experienced the day before, on her birthday. Between her talk with Roseanne and making amends with Yoshiko, she felt better than she had in weeks. Even at her morning classes—Spanish and Europe from 1815—she felt as if she were more awake, more attentive. It still made her sad to think about her breakup with Damon, but Jenna really felt like she was moving on.

Lunch with a handsome thirtyish police detective upon whom she had once had a massive crush that she still sort of nurtured . . . well, that didn't hurt either.

They sat at a small table at Espresso's, eating pepperoni-and-mushroom pizza. Danny broached the subject of the Alan Nash murder even before Jenna could ask, and she prodded him for more information. She was just as eager to hear about the case as he was to tell her.

"It's quite a mystery, isn't it?" she asked. "I mean, how do you burn someone to death in public and not have anyone notice?"

"You love a mystery, don't you?" Danny asked admiringly.

"I don't know if *love* is the right word," she said, glancing away. "I enjoy a challenge, though." Jenna felt the words catch in her throat, afraid that Danny might have taken them the wrong way, as though there were some innuendo in that sentence. She glanced up at him, but he seemed unfazed, which was good. "Do you . . . have any suspects?"

Danny glanced around, apparently concerned that someone might overhear, but the tables around them were empty. Espresso's specialized in delivery, and Monday lunch was a quiet time.

"The girlfriend," he admitted. "Doing a background check right now. And one of the witnesses is kind of a strange character. The problem is, we still have to figure out how it was done before we can officially call it a murder."

Jenna grunted and nodded thoughtfully.

In the moment of silence that followed, she *felt* the tone of their conversation change; even the energy that flowed between them was altered. Jenna frowned and studied Danny's face, searching for an explanation.

"So . . . about the other day," he said. "You seem a little better now, but I just thought you were pretty out of sorts. Figured you could use someone to talk to."

Jenna smiled. "I am feeling a little better, actually. It's so sweet that you worry about me. Truly. I guess it's just . . . you know Damon and I broke up, and I took it harder than I thought I would. I let it kind of haunt me, I guess."

"Why'd you guys break up?"

Startled by the frankness of the question, Jenna flinched. "Um, that's . . . it's . . ."

"I'm sorry," Danny muttered, waving a hand in front of him. "None of my business."

Jenna could see how uncomfortable he had become suddenly, and she didn't want that. Not at all. "No, it's okay," she told him. "I just . . . I haven't really been talking to anyone about it. That's all."

Danny nodded. It was clearly okay with him if she did not want to discuss it. But as she looked at him, she realized that she *did* want him to know, that she felt like she should tell *someone*. When the words started to come out, she was stunned to find out how few there were. How simple it all really was.

"I guess what it comes down to is that he just doesn't *get* me. Doesn't understand why I do what I do and why it's so important to me. He wants to live what he thinks is a normal life, and what I do just isn't normal enough for him, I guess. *I'm* not normal enough. He didn't want to deal with that."

Danny started to laugh.

"Hey!" Jenna protested, anger and embarrassment rising up in her. "I don't think it's very—"

Danny reached out and grabbed her hands, holding them tightly in his own, his laughter trailing off as his stormy blue eyes grew serious again.

"No, hey, no," he said, his voice low and tender. "I wasn't laughing at you, Jenna. It's just . . ." He hesitated, shook his head once. "That just sounds a little too familiar, you know what I'm saying? You're a different case because you're in college, and your job is just part of who you are; but for cops, for anyone who does the kinds of things we both do, it is really difficult to find someone who understands how intense it can all be, how important it seems. No, to hell with that, how important it *is*. With all I've seen, I've had people ask me how I can sleep at night. The answer is simple. The only way I can sleep is if I know I've done everything I can."

Jenna's mouth went suddenly dry as she stared into Danny's eyes. It was a very powerful thing to know that she was not alone.

"Look, anytime you need to talk to someone or just go out and blow off steam or whatever . . . I'm that guy for you. Whenever you need me," Danny promised, and held her hands more tightly.

Jenna was about to speak, but then she flinched and pulled away from him as though his touch had burned her. She stared at him, emotion welling in the back of her throat, rising in her chest.

Danny's expression was completely mystified. "Jenna, what—"

"Don't be too nice to me," she said quickly, interrupting him.

"What? I don't understand."

Jenna swallowed, forcing herself to breathe regularly, getting over the rush of emotions she had felt just moments before. Once she had her composure back, she met his gaze directly, chin high.

"I'm still hurting, Danny. I don't want you to be too nice to me because I still have feelings for you, and it might get my hopes up, and then I'll just get hurt all over again."

Danny blinked and sat back in his chair, obviously completely flustered. He started to reply a couple of times, his hands moving around as though trying to build an answer. Finally he shook his head.

"I guess I really don't know what to say to that, Jenna," he confessed. "I care about you a lot. Maybe more than I should. Maybe more than is appropriate," Danny told her, voice low, eyes deep and blue as the sea and searching her own. "I admire you more than you can imagine. You're the most unique girl I've ever met. But in the real world, I'm not sure that's enough. There are reasons why we can't be more involved than we are. I know you understand that. But it makes me sad to think all that might prevent us from being friends."

Jenna smiled softly, sadly. "It won't," she said. "I promise."

But later, when Danny drove away from the curb in front of Espresso's, and Jenna started her walk back up the hill to campus, she remembered the way that she felt when Danny had held her hands and spoken so eloquently about bittersweet truths. It made her both sad and happy to know that Danny cared so much for her.

More than he should, she reminded herself.

Jenna thought about Damon and Yoshiko and Roseanne and everything that had happened over the previous few weeks, and she sighed deeply, laughed at herself, and kept walking.

"Life goes on," she whispered, just loud enough, so that only she could hear.

It was too easy.

There was still a kind of wonderfully horrid glee in the killing, but the simplicity of it gave him a sense of omnipotence that he knew was both false and dangerous. If he grew too arrogant, he would make a mistake, perhaps a fatal one. Fortunately, it hurt him to burn them. Perverse as it was, he appreciated that pain for the reminder it provided: This is not without cost. This is not without effort and peril, the hazard of discovery.

Perhaps it would have been wiser to break into a home or office when no one else was around, to kill in secrecy. But it was so much less complicated to do it out on the street, simply passing by, when any bystander might be a suspect. And he had to confess to himself that he was a bit of an exhibitionist. Committing murder in public, in full view of dozens, or even hundreds, of people, and getting away with it—watching the faces of the witnesses—it was all such a rush that he could not bring himself to hide what he did.

It hurt him to call upon the fire within; it hurt to burn them.

But in those seconds after, when the screaming started and he could smell the searing flesh and watch horror sculpting the faces of those around him, those few seconds made up for any pain he might feel.

Late Monday afternoon, on the cusp of evening, he stood across the street from the glass-and-steel tower that housed the advertising agency where Kendall Sobler worked. At twelve minutes past five o'clock exactly, Kendall exited the building, purse slung over her shoulder. She wore slimming brown pants and a heavy jacket with a beige blouse beneath, and white Nike sneakers on her feet. In downtown Boston, that was the uniform of the working woman. Kendall would have several pairs of shoes, at least, stashed in a drawer or under her desk at work, and she would slip into or out of them at the beginning and end of each day. But for the walk to and from work, the sneakers were invaluable.

Though she was almost startlingly attractive, with long, straight black hair, wide hazel eyes, and a mouth that seemed almost perpetually turned up into a pleasant smile, Kendall went unnoticed in the throng that made its exodus onto Congress Street in those minutes after five. The streets were flooded with people rushing home to spouses or children or a comfortable chair and a glass of wine.

That's what Kendall will have waiting for her, he thought. *She'll sip the wine, taking the time to wind down before fixing dinner. There'll be music on to keep her company. Something soft and heartbreaking.*

Or there would have been. If not for me.

He watched as Kendall shouldered her way through the crowd on the sidewalk—many moving toward the Quincy Market area, but far more heading for the subway—then cut across Congress Street between cars bumper to bumper at the lights. She went past a vendor selling flowers on a corner of Congress and State. Though she was harried now, he pictured Kendall relaxed at home, content among her things. Protected within her fortress walls.

He laughed softly to himself.

Then he set off after her, moving across the street to fall into step behind her as she hurried toward the door of State Street Station. She was a runner, true, but in this crush of humanity, there would be no running. As inconspicuously as he could manage, he moved through the crowd, a bit faster than Kendall, a bit less concerned about who he nudged aside, a bit more imposing as he did so. Nobody noticed. They were used to being jostled.

There was a second street vendor—this one selling roasted nuts—outside the T station doors. A crowd of people waited patiently to squeeze through the narrow entrance, and Kendall joined them. He moved behind her. They were all so close he could smell cologne and perfume and cigarette smoke and bad breath and body odor even over the smell of the roasting nuts. Nobody was looking down.

He slid his hand forward. In order to be sure he was not seen, he kept his hand low. His fingers grazed the soft fabric that covered her butt, then he pulled them away immediately.

"Hey!" Kendall protested.

She scowled and tried to turn around, but it was nearly her turn to enter, and the press of people around her would not allow her to deviate from that course.

Then, with a sound not unlike banging on a large, hollow drum, she burst into flame. The fire touched the clothes of those around her, and they all began screaming. The crowd scattered, people batting at their jackets and skirts. At first Kendall was just one of them, though her screams were louder than the others.

Then the screams were *about* her. Commuters stared in horror as her face turned black and her hair blazed like a woodpile set alight. Kendall tried to run, tried to find some way to put out the blaze. That lasted for only a few seconds. Then she fell to her knees on the sidewalk, near the wide-eyed, green-faced nut vendor, and started thrashing on the ground as she burned. Her skull struck the pavement several times with sickening *thuds*. When her eyes boiled in their sockets and burst, there were more screams. The nut vendor vomited onto his cart.

Kendall Sobler's corpse lay smoldering on the sidewalk with the sound of approaching ambulance sirens wailing in the distance. The rubber on the soles of her white Nikes had begun to bubble and melt onto the pavement.

It was seventeen minutes past five o'clock on Monday.

Rush hour.

chapter 4

It was almost six o'clock in the evening, and Danny was exhausted. With two hours still remaining in his shift, he was more than ready to knock off for the day. If he couldn't go home yet, he at least wanted to be out on the street, doing his job. *Anything* was better than sitting at the desk in his cluttered office, hunched over a keyboard, and typing up the report of the incident he and Audrey had investigated earlier that day.

Even with such a clear open-and-shut case of domestic violence leading to murder—in this instance, it was the husband who hadn't gotten to the family gun fast enough and, thus, caught four of the six bullets his wife fired—there was still plenty of paperwork. Audrey had been working on it with him, but she was in the break room refilling their coffee cups when the telephone rang. Danny grabbed it before it could ring a second time.

Anything to avoid typing, he thought as he pressed the receiver to his ear. "Mariano," he snapped. It wasn't a public number, so he dispensed with the formalities.

"What are you doing playing desk jockey?" a low-pitched voice asked.

The sarcasm was obvious, and Danny instantly recognized the gruff voice of Lieutenant Hall Boggs of the Boston P.D. Homicide Division.

"What can I do for you, Lieutenant?" Danny asked.

Audrey appeared in the doorway, then shot him a questioning look as she walked over to place his cup of steaming coffee on the edge of his desk. Danny glanced up at her, nodded his thanks, and gave her a quick *I don't know yet* shrug.

"We've got something over here at the State Street T station that I thought you might like to take a look at," Boggs said. "I tried your lieutenant, but he wasn't in his office."

"What's the matter," Danny teased, "your guys can't handle it, so you decided to get some *professional* help?"

Boggs's snorting sounded more like an animal grunting than a human being laughing. Then he cleared his throat. "Oh, we can handle it all right. Just exhibiting a little professional courtesy. Woman we've got here looks a lot like that burn victim you had out your way last week."

Danny frowned and shifted forward in his chair, totally alert now. Catching his reaction, Audrey took a step closer.

"I thought maybe you'd like to check it out," Boggs continued, "see if there's anything that might connect this one with yours."

"We'll be right there," Danny said, feeling a tight hitch in his chest. He hung up quickly and looked at Audrey.

"Burn victim at the State Street Station," he said. "Looks like the same M.O." Without another word, they grabbed their coats and were out the door.

Although most of the evening rush hour traffic had disappeared by six o'clock, the drive from Somerset to Boston still took longer than either Danny or Audrey liked. Forty-five minutes after the phone on Danny's desk had rung, they pulled up to the crime scene at the T station on the corner of State Street. Danny had always thought it an odd place to put a subway station, in the basement of a handsome colonial-era brick building.

The crime scene perimeter was marked by bright yellow POLICE LINE: DO NOT CROSS tape strung between orange sawhorses. He counted nine police cruisers along with two ambulances and several fire trucks, all with their red and blue emergency lights flashing. In the gathering dark, the light created a disorienting strobe effect, but Danny had experienced it so many times before that he hardly noticed. A large crowd of curious onlookers had gathered but were being held back by police officers, and the snarl of traffic at the intersection was a commuter's worst nightmare.

Danny parked at an angle to the curb and threw

the POLICE BUSINESS tag onto his dashboard before getting out. Audrey took the lead, and they made their way through the crowd. Boggs spotted them, and Danny nodded a silent greeting as the Boston homicide lieutenant moved their way.

"Good to see you, Lieutenant," Audrey said stiffly.

Boggs stuck out a hand to shake. "Detective Gaines," he said.

The two had never hit it off. Not that anyone ever likely hit it off with Hall Boggs, a brick wall of a man with a brusque manner. Danny knew it would be up to him to do the talking.

"So what have you got?" Danny asked, rubbing his hands together. The night was cold, and in his haste he had forgotten his gloves.

A noxious, smoky stench lingered in the air and made him cough. He recognized it from that night at DePasquale Brothers and knew that it wasn't just exhaust fumes from the cars or trains. He saw that Audrey was covering her nose with her clenched fist; she smelled it, too.

"This way," Boggs said, with a quick sideways twitch of his head.

Danny and Audrey followed a few steps behind him. The closer they got to where the police, firefighters, and emergency med-techs were gathered, the stronger the burned-hair smell got. Danny's stomach was churning even before he saw the charred corpse lying on the ground. There wasn't much left. The victim—whoever it was—looked like little more than a human-shaped mound of gray, brittle ash. Danny had the impression that it was hollow and would collapse inward if anyone even touched it.

The corpse looked female, but Danny couldn't be sure. The body was lying on its left side in a fetal position, legs up and arms clutched tightly against the chest. She—yeah, now he was pretty sure it was a woman—had been shrunk by the consuming flames, so that now she was not much larger than a child. The clothes were singed beyond recognition. Her eye sockets were dark, empty holes with traces of brown, crusted residue where blood and vitreous fluid had run down the cheeks.

"Got any ID yet?" Audrey asked. Her voice caught just a little.

Danny had not been able to speak right away, afraid that his voice would give him away. Now he realized that the corpse and the stench were getting to Audrey just as much as they were to him. She could not help the tiny hitch in her voice, but that was all she would allow herself. He was her partner; nobody else would have even noticed.

Boggs cocked his head to one side, scratched his unshaven cheek and nodded.

"Her purse wasn't completely torched. Looks like maybe she dropped it as soon as she . . . went up. Trying to beat out the flames or whatever. Name's Kendall Sobler. Works over at Cragmore Advertising."

"Kendall?" Danny said, frowning. "Isn't that usually a man's name?"

"Hey, I don't name 'em," Boggs snapped, "I just

tag 'em and bag 'em. I've got a call in to the M.E. He's on the way."

Danny wondered if the M.E. that Boggs was referring to would be a pathologist from Massachusetts General or Boston City Hospital, or if they had called on Walter Slikowski. Slick was the county medical examiner, but Boston P.D. tended not to call him to the scene, leaving it to others to do the on-site and only calling on Slick to look at paperwork and consult on special cases.

On the other hand, Slick was already on this case, and Boggs had called Danny with the news. It would only make sense for him to call on the county M.E.'s expertise.

Danny glanced at Audrey over his shoulder, feeling almost guilty for wondering if perhaps Jenna would accompany Dr. Slikowski on this run. He hoped she would. One of the other officers called out to Boggs, who nodded a silent good-bye to Audrey and Danny before turning to leave.

"I'll start running down everything I can on the victim," Audrey told him, once they were in the car. "See if we've got a connection to Nash or his girl-friend."

"Yeah," Danny said grimly, "and I'll see if I can locate Victor Frost. Gotta wonder if he's got an alibi for the last couple of hours."

"You make him for this one?" Audrey asked, arching one eyebrow.

"Got anything better?" Danny asked.

*   *   *

"Hey!" Jenna said brightly as she rushed over to the table where Roseanne sat. "Sorry I'm late. Trying to get caught up on a couple of Spanish assignments. I've been falling behind in that class."

The Campus Center dining area was crowded at lunchtime, but Roseanne had commandeered a small table over by the windows that looked out toward the distant gray, late-winter skyline of Boston.

"You're not late," Roseanne said. "I got here a little early and was too hungry to wait."

"No prob," Jenna said. "Feeling pretty ravenous myself." With a smile, she sat down and slid her tray onto the table. She had a plate of lasagna with Italian bread, a glass of Coke, and a small bowl of salad. Her stomach rumbled.

"You're all Tigger-y today," Roseanne said pleasantly, studying Jenna. "Did you just get some good news or something?"

"No," Jenna replied as she opened her napkin and spread it on her lap. Then she shrugged. "Just feeling good, I guess. The days are getting a little longer. A little warmer. Spring may not be in the air, but it's peeking around the corner."

"See?" Roseanne said, her smile widening. "I told you that getting a little exercise would be good for you."

"Oh, it's not just that," Jenna said. "It's a whole bunch of things. I'm telling you, ever since my birthday—"

Jenna couldn't help but notice that Roseanne frowned slightly as she looked up quickly. The motion made her hair bob at her shoulders.

"I didn't know it was your birthday," she said. "When was that?"

"Oh, just a couple of days ago," Jenna said with a casual wave of her hand. "Yeah—the big *one-nine*. I didn't want to make a big deal about it or anything. Just my mom and I went out for supper."

"Oh, I see," Roseanne said.

For just an instant, Jenna thought she detected a trace of hurt in her friend's eyes, but she let it pass. She was feeling too good to let anything bother her. She had plans to hang out with Yoshiko and Hunter later that night. They had talked about hitting a party at the AOPi sorority but Jenna was not sure she was up for that. What she really wanted was a chance for her and her friends to get off campus together so they could just be themselves—the three *amigos*.

"You know, we—" Jenna started to say, but then she cut herself off.

"Huh?" Roseanne asked, eyebrows arched as she paused with a forkful of salad halfway to her mouth.

Jenna didn't say anything right away. Instead, she took a bite of Italian bread and chewed thoughtfully for a moment. She had been about to tell Roseanne about her plans for that night, and to invite her new friend along with them. But almost instantly she decided against it. She had no doubt that Hunter and Yoshiko would like Roseanne—and she was enjoying getting to know her new friend better—but tonight was going to be just for the three of them.

"No, I—I was just going to say I think we should get together to study for that Medical Anthro exam that's coming up next week," Jenna said, hoping she covered quickly enough.

"I can use all the help I can get," Roseanne said, shaking her head and rolling her eyes. "I got a C on the last quiz. How'd you do?"

"I did all right," Jenna replied, lowering her gaze. "A minus."

"Ohh, I hate you," Roseanne said, swatting her hand at Jenna with an evil little chuckle. "You're such a brainiac. Some of us actually have to sweat the work, y'know."

Jenna raised her eyebrows with an apologetic smile, even as she studied Roseanne more closely. She could not have said exactly what it was about the girl, but Roseanne definitely reminded her of Melody LaChance. They didn't look anything alike, but there was an easy way about Roseanne, a confidence and charisma that Melody'd also had. Of course, thoughts of Melody's murder the previous semester put an instant damper on Jenna's good feelings, but she hid it well and after a while it passed.

"Seriously, Jenna, how do you do it?" Roseanne asked. "You work at the medical center and go to college full time, and still make time for a life."

"I don't know," Jenna said. It was an honest answer, for she had not really ever considered the question before. "I don't worry too much about studying. I mean I do it, of course, but I don't let myself get too stressed about it. I don't have time to worry. Maybe that's the key, y'know? With all the nasty things I see at work, and how intense that can get, I don't have the ability to second-guess my study habits anymore. I do my best, and that's that."

Roseanne shook her head, lips pressed together in a thin smile. "You're something else. All that stuff is supposed to make it harder for you to do well in school, not easier."

"Guess I'm just lucky," Jenna replied.

"I guess," Roseanne teased. "Spending all that time with dead people. What luck. I don't know how you can do that for work. Do you actually enjoy being in a morgue?"

"Well, it's not the morgue, exactly. But, yeah, I really do," Jenna said. She smiled and took a deep breath. "I'll try to explain that to you sometime, but you're not the only friend who doesn't understand me because of that."

"Well, to each her own, I guess," Roseanne said, still looking a bit mystified.

The girls ate their lunch and talk turned to other subjects. When Jenna had to leave, Roseanne seemed disappointed, but made no move to get up.

"I think I'll just sit here a while longer . . . maybe get another cup of coffee and just watch the world go by."

"Always a good plan," Jenna said, smiling. "Let me get this for you." She picked up Roseanne's tray and balanced it on her own, then stood up.

"So, maybe tomorrow we can hit the old Medical Anthro books, huh?" Roseanne asked brightly.

"Absolutely," Jenna replied.

She glanced at the clock and realized that she was

going to have to hurry if she didn't want to be late for work. After a quick good-bye, she hurried up the hill, heading back to Sparrow Hall. She ran up the stairs, taking them two at a time to the third floor. Jenna was a little winded from the exertion as she rounded the corner and started down the hallway toward her room.

Damon was walking toward her. Jenna's good mood evaporated instantly.

She stiffened as they locked eyes. There was no way to avoid each other, and as they got closer, she forced herself to smile despite the cold, sharp jab in the center of her chest and the sour lump forming in her throat.

"Hey. How's it going?" Damon asked. He stopped in front of her, a tentative, hopeful smile on his face.

"Great . . . just great," Jenna replied, finding it difficult to look him in the eye.

"Cool. I'm glad to hear it," Damon said. His smile took on an aspect that might have been panic, or maybe just awkwardness.

Tension tightened Jenna's jaw. It felt so odd not to embrace him, to kiss him, the way she would have only a handful of weeks ago. They stood there facing each other and Jenna had no idea what to say or do next. She could see by his expression and the way he was shifting his weight from one foot to the other that this was just as awkward for him as it was for her.

One question burned in her mind, and seeing him so unexpectedly like this made her realize that it was the only question she still wanted to ask him. *How could you do that to me? How could you cheat on me like that with Caitlin?*

Instead, all she could manage was "And you?"

"I'm good," Damon replied with a tiny shrug.

Of course you are, Jenna thought as her feelings of discomfort blended into anger and hurt. *You got exactly what you wanted. Maybe you had to do it by cheating on me, but you definitely got what you wanted!*

"Well, I ought to get going. Got to get to work," Jenna said. She hoped that her voice didn't betray the tangle of emotions she was feeling.

"Yeah," Damon said, frowning a bit. "How's that going?"

"Fine," Jenna told him, well aware that her job had been a major factor in the ending of their relationship. "Listen, Damon, I'll see you later, okay?"

"Yeah. You take care."

As she walked away from Damon, she could hear the soft scuff of his sneakers on the carpeted floor. The hair on the back of her neck prickled, and her face felt hot and flushed. She was tempted to turn and take one last look at him, but she didn't know which would hurt more—seeing that he had also stopped to look back at her or realizing that he had walked away without another thought.

"So where are we going?" Jenna asked as she started up the car and backed it out of the parking slot. Yoshiko was in the front seat next to her, so Hunter had the back to himself. He leaned forward far enough to poke his head between them as he rested his chin on his folded arms on the back of the front seat, in total defiance of seat belt laws.

"Why don't we drive out to Revere Beach?" Hunter offered. "My roommate was telling me about this place called Kelly's that's supposed to have the best fried clams in New England."

"Fried clams?" Yoshiko said, wrinkling her nose. "I didn't know you liked fried clams."

"I don't, really," Hunter said with just a touch of defensiveness in his voice. "I was just saying, if we were looking for something completely different to do, it might be fun to drive out to the beach."

"And *now* for something *completely* different," Jenna said in a faux Monty Python accent as she turned left onto College Avenue, heading toward Kettle Square.

"Don't you think it might be jumping the gun just a little bit to be going out to the beach in the middle of March?" Yoshiko asked with a frown.

"Umm, maybe just a bit," Jenna said, but she was up for an adventure simply because it was so different from anything they usually did together. "I have heard about Kelly's, though. Kelly's Roast Beef, it's called, though I heard the thing about the clams, too. My mom and I used to go up to Farnam's in Ipswich. They were also supposed to have the best clams, but Kelly's is kind of legendary around here."

"Hello, the *beach*," Yoshiko reminded them. "I mean, if I was back home in Hawaii, I could see it. But I'm still not used to this New England weather. No one's planning to take a little swim, are they?

Because if you are, I'm afraid I left my swimsuit back at the dorm."

"What a shame," Hunter said with a lascivious grin. "You'll have to go without."

"It's freezing!" Yoshiko protested. Grinning, she turned slightly in her seat and whacked him on the head with the flat of her hand.

Hunter barely flinched. "And if it wasn't?" he asked.

"We'll have to talk about that when it's warmer," Yoshiko replied mischievously.

"Ah!" Jenna cried. "I am not hearing this! I am not listening!"

"So you're up for it?" Hunter asked brightly. The prospect of food seemed always to get his attention.

"Sure, why not?" Yoshiko said, "but if Kelly's is supposed to be so great for fried clams, why do they have *roast beef* in their name?"

"I have no idea," Hunter said with a shrug, "but let's give it a try."

"Sounds good to me," Jenna said as she negotiated the curve of the rotary. "I've never been to Revere Beach before, so I'm not exactly sure how to get there. We just go out on Route Sixteen, don't we?"

"Sounds good to me," Hunter said, "just so long as we stop someplace soon so we can eat. I'm feeling a little hollow."

"Are you sure that's not your head you're talking about?" Jenna asked, and all three of them burst into laughter. Hunter gave her a playful swat on the shoulder.

"Mom!" Jenna whined in a little-girl voice, "Hunter's hitting me!"

They continued to tease one another as the radio rumbled low, just beneath their voices. Soundtrack to their lives. Barenaked Ladies gave way to Sting and then to Dave Matthews.

The night sky was dark, but so far the storm that had been threatening all day had not come. As she drove, Jenna felt really content, happy just to be with her two friends. It felt like it used to, before the thing with Damon had started to go bad. No one was sure where to go, so they got lost a few times on the way, and Hunter's complaints that he was getting hungry took on a more serious note. Eventually they found Revere Beach Avenue, and after driving up the road for a mile or so with the churning, gray Atlantic Ocean on their right, Jenna saw a small, brightly lit, brick-fronted building on the left.

"I'm guessing that's it," she said, pointing down the road.

Even in the cold and dark, they could see a short line of people huddled against the cold as they waited outside the opened window to place their orders.

"Are they completely wacko?" Yoshiko said, amazed.

"Fruity as a nutcake," Hunter confirmed. "But no more than we are."

"Yeah, but—I mean, with the ocean and all it can't be more than thirty degrees out there. I can't believe *anyone* would wait in line outside in this weather . . . especially for fried clams."

"Must be *really* good clams," Hunter said with an exaggerated smacking of his lips.

Jenna saw an empty parking spot across the street from Kelly's and pulled into it. As she did, her head-lights washed across the sandy stretch of beach and illuminated the white surf that was rolling onto the shore.

"Man, oh, *man!*" Hunter said. "Now I really wish I had brought my bathing suit."

"If you're not careful, Yoshiko and I just might throw you in," Jenna offered. When she opened her door and stepped outside, a frigid blast of wind caught the door and almost knocked her back into the car.

"Make sure to wait half an hour after we eat," Hunter retorted.

He scrambled out the back door and did the south-ern gentleman thing, opening the door for Yoshiko with a flourish and a bow. She pulled her hat down and the collar of her jacket up to her ears as she stepped out into the night.

"I may never forgive you for this," she said between chattering teeth as the three of them ran across the road and took their place in line.

The wind had a salty chill that cut through coats and scarves and mittens and gloves. It was worse standing in line, and they all bounced and jogged in place trying to keep warm. By the time they were ready to place their orders, they were all shivering so badly they had a little trouble telling the woman working the window what they wanted. Once they got their food—a half pint of clams each, sodas, and a pint of onion rings to share—and were back in the car, Jenna started it up so the heater could run while they ate.

Yoshiko gingerly dipped a clam into a paper cup filled with tartar sauce and took a cautious bite. Her eyes widened.

"Umm . . . these are *really* good," she confessed.

Hunter was so busy scarfing his half pint in the backseat that he only managed a mumbled response. Feeling absolutely content, Jenna settled back behind the steering wheel and ate slowly as she looked out at the churning surf. She was surprised when she saw two figures walking hand in hand down the beach toward them.

"Now *that's* what I call true love," Yoshiko said when she noticed them. "Going for a romantic walk on the beach on a night like this."

"Love or insanity," Hunter muttered, barely looking up from his food.

"What's the difference?" Jenna asked, no trace of humor in her tone.

Neither of her friends responded to that one.

"You know," Jenna said after a while, "I was thinking about asking Roseanne if she'd like to come along with us tonight, but I'm kind of glad I didn't. It's really good to have it be just the . . . the three of us."

She had almost said *four*. Though she had not been thinking about him while driving around with Hunter and Yoshiko, her run-in with Damon was apparently still fresh in her mind.

"Hey," Yoshiko said, concern in her tone. "You all right? You could have brought her, you know."

"It isn't that," Jenna replied. "It's . . . I ran into Damon today. I guess it's still bugging me."

Yoshiko and Hunter were silent as they waited for her to continue.

Jenna looked back out at the ocean. "I wanted to ask him about Caitlin, but I just couldn't get up the guts. It's just . . . Damon and I are over, I know that, and I'm actually cooler with it now than I thought I would be. But the thought that he cheated on me with Caitlin is just . . ."

As soon as it was out, she regretted saying it. It was just her own nasty paranoia working, and what was the point? *Move on,* she told herself. And she wanted to, but this one thing was just gnawing at her.

The car seat made a loud creaking sound as Hunter shifted forward. Jenna felt his hand come to rest lightly on her shoulder and give her a reassuring squeeze.

"Hey, J," he said, his voice husky with emotion, "if it's any help, I've talked to both Olivia and Brick since then, and Damon didn't do anything with Caitlin until you two had broken up. Those two would know."

"Caitlin wouldn't have done that to you," Yoshiko told her, "even if Damon would have, which I doubt." She reached out and placed her hand gently on top of Jenna's. "And I don't know if this helps or not, but they aren't seeing each other anymore."

Jenna felt like crying, but her eyes were dry. She shook her head. "Thanks, you guys. You know, it's weird; that should make me feel better, but somehow it doesn't."

Turning to face them, Jenna still had her hand on the back of the driver's seat with Yoshiko's on top of hers. Hunter reached up and laid his hand on theirs, too.

c h a p t e r 5

On Wednesday afternoon, as she trod the familiar
path from Sparrow Hall, through the academic quad
and across Carpenter Street to Somerset Medical
Center, Jenna found herself filled with a kind of morbid curiosity. It occurred to her that morbid was just
about the only kind of curiosity available at her job,
and she chuckled to herself.

One of these days, she thought, *I'm going to be just a
little too morbid for polite company.*

The night before she had seen a report on the local
news about the burning death of Kendall Sobler. It
sounded to her an awful lot like the murder of Alan
Nash the previous week, the case that had Danny and
Audrey running ragged at the moment. The Sobler
woman had died in Boston. While that did not necessarily mean the county M.E. would be the one to do
the autopsy, the really nasty ones usually ended up
with Slick, or at least with the police consulting him.

But Jenna had been at work the day before and heard nary a peep about Kendall Sobler. Sure, Slick had been doing rounds at the various county hospitals that day, but she was still surprised they had heard nothing.

Curious.

Jenna strode confidently along the path in front of SMC, enthusiastic about work, pleased with the way things had gone with Yoshiko and Hunter the night before, and just generally feeling good about herself. That morning, before Gross Anatomy, she had taken the time to look really good, to put more effort into fixing her hair than she had in recent weeks, and to choose an outfit that would make her feel even more on top of things. In black jeans and shoes, an olive turtleneck, and her hip-length black leather coat, she knew she looked great.

It felt wonderful.

Girl with a mission, she went into the medical center and rode the elevator up to the second floor, where Slick had his office. Down a short hall in the administration wing, she used her key card to buzz the lock open and pushed in through the door.

Jenna blew out a little breath that verged on sigh territory. The outer office was deserted, and she felt a bit disappointed. If Slick and Dyson weren't around, that meant mostly transcription and paperwork for her today. Dr. Slikowski's office door was not open all the way, but the room was silent and that was enough to tell her he was not there. If he had been, jazz would have been flowing from the Bose sound system in that interior office. Probably Joshua Redman or Dexter Gordon, as both had been in the CD player pretty regularly for the past week or so. New and old, Slick just loved jazz.

Resigned to life at the keyboard, Jenna began to slip off her jacket.

"Hello?"

With a start, she turned to see Natalie Kerchak standing in the doorway to Slick's office. The previous day's gray skies had burned off and the sun shone through the windows now, silhouetting the woman and bringing fire to her long red hair.

"Oh, Jenna, it's you," Natalie said, her tone filled with genuine warmth.

"Natalie, hi," Jenna quickly replied. "You scared me. I didn't think anyone was here."

"Dr. Dyson went downstairs to prepare for an autopsy," the woman explained. "He said I could wait here for Walter. Apparently he had a lecture at the medical school, which he neglected to mention when he asked me to stop by for lunch."

"Men," Jenna said with a roll of her eyes.

"All of them," Natalie agreed sagely.

They both laughed.

Jenna hung up her jacket as Natalie came farther out into the main office. Her eyes seemed to sparkle with life, and Jenna found herself thinking how beautiful Natalie was. Her own mother was an attractive woman, or so Jenna had always believed. Natalie was fortyish, perhaps ten years younger than April Blake, but Jenna thought that the woman had a kind of easy energy that made her seem even younger. For a moment Jenna searched for a word to describe Natalie. The only one that came to mind was glamorous, but that wasn't quite right.

Close enough, she thought.

"So tell me," Natalie said, "what's going on between you and Detective Danny?"

Jenna stiffened, then looked at Natalie with wide eyes.

"Oh," the woman said, alarmed. "I'm sorry. I hope I didn't hit a sore point. I didn't really know there was anything happening. It's only that I saw the way you two were talking at your birthday party Saturday, and I assumed. Guess I shouldn't have."

"It's all right," Jenna said, shaking off her surprise. "You just caught me off-guard."

Natalie was watching her closely, but somehow Jenna did not feel as though she were being grilled. Not like with her mother. Once upon a time she had been able to tell April everything in her life without being afraid her mom would try to help work things out for her. Direct traffic. This was like that. Okay, Natalie was being a bit nosy, but Jenna thought it was more about making conversation. Being friendly.

It was surprisingly okay.

"There's an attraction there," Jenna confirmed. "He's . . . I've always had kind of a crush on him."

"From the look of things the other day, I don't think you're alone in that," Natalie told her.

Jenna flushed a bit, felt the warmth in her cheeks as they reddened. "Maybe. I'd like to think that's true.

But it doesn't really matter. He's so much older and it isn't like he'd be real interested in hanging out at campus parties and stuff. He's a cop all the time, but what I do around here? That's only part of my life. Plus, how would it look to the other detectives, him dating a college girl? My mother always says you can't fight fate."

"She's a wise woman, your mother," Natalie replied.

There was a wistful look on her face and she glanced once at the office door before returning her attention to Jenna. Her expression grew more serious.

"I've known Walter a long time," she confided. "He's very dedicated to his work."

Jenna felt uncomfortable talking about Slick behind his back, but she could not help putting voice to the question that sprang to mind. "Is that a problem?"

"Once it was," Natalie admitted. "We dated before. I'm not sure if he told you that or not. It was a long time ago. Back then, he was already too serious about his work, spent too much time on it, let it get inside him. He carried it around with him all the time. He's still serious about the job. A workaholic, as if you didn't know."

The woman paused, scrutinized Jenna. "Don't let him do that to you, Jenna. Don't let him turn you into that. He's a very good man and an excellent example in many ways, but not in that one.

"Anyway, as I said, he still cares profoundly about

his work," Natalie went on. "But it doesn't consume him anymore. I saw that the moment we began to see each other again. It's the thing that is going to allow this relationship to work. Walter knows there is more to life than the job, that there are other priorities.

"I'm not suggesting anything in regard to your feelings for Danny, except that perhaps when you're so deeply entrenched in something, it's hard to see beyond the people who are in the trenches with you. There's a world outside the job for all of you."

The office door buzzed and then was pushed open as Dr. Slikowski wheeled his chair inside. He frowned as he saw them, and Jenna was sure that he was puzzled by their conspiratorial smiles.

"Hello, Walter," Natalie began.

"I know, I'm late," Slick said quickly. He held up a hand to forestall any recriminations. "Forgive me. My students cry out for inspiration."

Natalie shot him a reproachful look. "Right."

"Okay, they pumped me for information about the upcoming boards, and I led them to believe that they could not survive without my wisdom," Slick confessed, feigning shame.

"That's more like it," Natalie said. "The unadorned truth. Where are we going for lunch?"

Now all trace of humor left Slick's face. He took a breath, a guilty, haunted look in his eyes.

"It's all right," Natalie told him. "Dyson already told me about this autopsy. I know it's important. Shall we just go down to Au Bon Pain for a quick bite?"

Jenna had never seen her employer so relieved.

"You're something else," Slick told Natalie. Then he turned his attention to Jenna. "Would you mind going downstairs and letting Dyson know I'll be another forty-five minutes? Then we'll get started."

"No problem," Jenna said. Then, with a quick wave and a warm smile for Natalie, she went quickly out of the office and headed for the autopsy room in the basement.

When she stepped out of the elevator and started down the corridor, Jenna spotted Dyson at the far end of the hall rolling a gurney out of the morgue. The cadaver he was in the midst of transporting into the autopsy room was covered with a sheet, but looked so small to Jenna that it might have been the corpse of a child. The victim this time was a woman, she had known that. But Jenna also understood that the smallness that unnerved her so much came not merely from the diminutive stature of the dead woman, but from the fact that she had died in fire.

Fire lessened its victims. Diminished them. If the blaze was bad enough, what remained hardly looked human anymore. That had been the case with Alan Nash, and she knew it would be the case here as well.

Jenna shuddered.

With his shoulder, Dyson nudged open the door to autopsy. He propped it awkwardly with one outstretched foot as he trundled the gurney inside.

"Want some help?" Jenna asked as she approached.

Dyson glanced up at her, smiled pleasantly. "Love some. Doing this myself is always a little like a morbid game of Twister."

"You could always prop it open with the door-stop," Jenna observed, grinning mischievously. "You know, the one that's there specifically for that purpose?"

"I could," Dyson agreed. He shot her a withering glance. "But that would take all the fun out of it. You gonna help or not?"

Jenna reached past the back end of the gurney and held the door open so that Dyson was free to wheel it into the autopsy room's sterile, stainless-steel environment.

"No rush getting her up on the table," Jenna told him. "Slick wanted me to tell you he's going to be another forty-five minutes or so."

Dyson looked at her quizzically.

"He promised Natalie he'd have lunch with her and doesn't want to end up in the doghouse," Jenna explained.

"Smart man," Dyson said. "Let's just put her in the cold room until he's ready."

Jenna helped him maneuver the gurney to the back of the autopsy room, open a large steel door, and wheel the cadaver into a much smaller room whose size and general design reminded Jenna of the beer coolers in the liquor store her grandfather had owned when she was a little girl. It was only about fifty degrees in "the cold room," but that was cold enough to store the cadaver until the autopsy would begin.

"Why didn't they autopsy her yesterday?" Jenna asked as they slid the gurney against one wall.

"They could have had a pathologist do it at BCH,"

Dyson replied. "But then Boston's Finest had a chat with Somerset P.D. and everyone agreed that the cause of death was too similar, that it had to be one case. BCH agreed that Slick should handle it since he did the first one. They shipped her over last night."

After the steel door was closed, Dyson leaned against it and looked steadily at Jenna. His eyes were haunted.

"What is it?" she asked.

Dyson shook his head slowly. "Nothing. Just . . . every time I see something that awful, I pray never to see anything like it again. It was horrifying enough that anybody had to die the way Alan Nash did. But now . . . well, once was bad, but twice is infinitely worse. Twice means there'll probably be more."

In the break room at Somerset police headquarters, Audrey Gaines sat across from Elena Manoff and kept her jaw firmly set. No trace of the excitement she felt was allowed to twitch at the corners of her mouth or cause her to raise her eyebrows.

"I hope I was able to be of some help," the woman said, a deep sadness in her brown eyes.

"Time will tell," Audrey replied. "I appreciate your coming in, Elena. I can reach you at work if we have any follow-up questions?"

The woman obviously realized she was being dismissed. She nodded in response to Audrey's question as she stood and slipped on her coat. At the door to the break room she turned and gazed at Audrey again.

"Kendall was not close to many people, Detective Gaines. I like to think I was one of them. She was quiet, a little shy around new people, but absolutely the kindest person I ever knew. She didn't deserve this."

"Nobody deserves what happened to your friend," Audrey assured her. "We'll catch whoever did this. When we do, they'll pay for it."

Elena Manoff glanced at the floor, gnawed her lip. "You can put them in prison for the rest of their lives and it won't be enough," she said. "Nobody can pay for Kendall. She was priceless. But at least you can make sure it doesn't happen to anyone else."

Audrey couldn't think of a single appropriate response. Wordlessly, she nodded and placed a comforting hand on the woman's shoulder. Elena turned and walked out into the squad room and Audrey followed. The woman did not even glance at the other people buzzing around the room. Danny stood leaning against his desk talking to Hall Boggs from Boston P.D., and the two hushed up as Audrey walked Elena past them.

Only when the woman had gone did Audrey return to them.

"What've you got?" Danny asked her instantly. "I can see it in your eyes."

Audrey regarded her partner coolly, then turned to Boggs. "Lieutenant. Good to see you again."

"Detective Gaines," Boggs replied with a nod.

"Audrey," Danny prodded. "Come on. You've got something. Spill."

"You first," Audrey replied, and nodded toward the two men. "You boys have been putting your heads together out here. What've you come up with?"

Boggs cleared his throat. "Why don't we go in and see your lieutenant for this?" he suggested.

The detectives agreed. They crossed the squad room to Lieutenant Gonci's office. He was just finishing with a phone call, and Audrey gave a soft knock on the door frame. Gonci waved them in as he hung up the phone and traded polite greetings with Boggs.

"So what've we got?" Gonci asked.

"While we've all been digging into the whys of this case, Boston P.D.'s been digging into the hows as well. I've got my team looking into every flammable substance and incendiary device available for commercial, industrial, or military use. Ever heard of Bernie Farchand?"

Audrey frowned. The name was familiar.

Danny snapped his fingers twice. "Yeah, yeah. The firebug, right? Did those arsons in Dorchester and Roxbury a couple of years ago."

Boggs nodded. "Probably the most talented arsonist in the country. If you can call that a talent. If anybody can tell us how this could be done, it's Farchand. We're trying to get him to agree to an interview now. Meanwhile, we're talking to a couple of armed forces experts as well. We're tracking known associates of both Alan Nash and Kendall Sobler, but have only just started with interviews and background checks, working in tandem with your squad. As for witnesses . . ."

The big man's words trailed off and he gestured toward Danny and Audrey. "But maybe your own detectives can tell you more about that. We've been working together, but you all had a head start on the witnesses from the Nash murder."

Gonci turned his gaze upon Danny and Audrey, but Audrey deferred to her partner. Danny had been the one following up on the witnesses; he had specifically asked for that end of the investigation.

"Detective Mariano?" Gonci inquired.

"Background checks on Mr. and Mrs. Randeau and Lizabeth Orton, the three who were dining together at DePasquale's the night of Nash's death, have all come up empty. They're local folks, no obvious connections, and again, they were there for a birthday. On the other hand, this Victor Frost is still a bit of a mystery. He could be completely on the up and up, but if you live in Cambridge, why go to a second-rate Italian restaurant in Somerset to try to meet women?

"Anyway, I'm running him down. Got a few calls in. So far all I know is he used to live in California. I'm running a DMV check and having someone in state gov out there do a search for priors. Until we hear back, I'd say we need to focus on the victims. Audrey just interviewed one of the Sobler woman's coworkers."

Gonci blinked, turned his attention to Audrey. They were all looking at her now and she held back the triumphant grin that threatened to break out at any second. It was a homicide investigation. Particularly grisly murders, too. Levity under those circumstances was hardly appropriate. Still, she could not prevent a tiny smile as she spoke.

"Elena Manoff. Works at Cragmore Advertising, the Sobler woman's place of employment," Audrey began. "Sobler was a receptionist there, Manoff works Human Resources. They had lunch together quite a bit. Manoff considered her a good friend, but I can't really tell how tight they were. Doesn't matter. We can learn what we need on follow-up. Key bit of information here is this. Most of her coworkers didn't know if Sobler was involved with anyone. But she told Manoff she was. Or had been, up until a few weeks ago, when things sort of fell apart. Apparently he was seeing someone else."

Gonci and Danny were staring at her intently. Boggs cleared his throat.

"Nash?" the big Boston cop asked.

Audrey nodded. "Nash."

chapter 6

Professor Finch's voice droned on and on as he described the biological functions of the human heart and some of the strange abnormalities that medical science had discovered over the years. Jenna usually enjoyed Gross Anatomy, but today there were too many other things on her mind distracting her.

The Friday morning class was just starting to study the circulatory system. Jenna had already read the chapter, partly because so much of it applied directly to her job. Unless Professor Finch got into some *really* weird abnormalities, she wasn't too sure he could add much to her basic knowledge of the structure of the human heart. Besides the professor, she was probably the only other person in the classroom who had actually held a human heart in her hands and sliced tissue samples from it.

If he's even done that, she thought, surprised at the

realization. *I could have more firsthand knowledge of this stuff than he does.*

Jenna shifted uncomfortably in her seat when she remembered how the hearts of the two burn victims she had helped autopsy recently had appeared slightly different. Dr. Slikowski had told her that was because the heart tissue had been "thoroughly roasted."

Talk about abnormalities, Jenna thought. *What kind of energy other than direct flame could incinerate a human body so badly that the internal organs were not at all burned, but were actually cooked?*

She shuddered at the thought and tried to force her attention back to what her professor was saying. Instead, she ended up leaning her chin on her hand and doodling in her notebook as Dr. Finch's words washed over her. After a while, she glanced at her watch, happy to see that the class was just about over.

"Well, I guess that's all for now," Dr. Finch said, glancing at his wristwatch and closing his lecture notes. "Remember for next class, you have to read chapter five in the text and be ready for a quiz on the similarities and differences in heart structure of cold-blooded and warm-blooded animals. See you next time."

Jenna jotted down the words "Heart Quiz" on the top of the page in her notebook before closing it and sliding it into her backpack. With the studying she needed to catch up on in Spanish and other assignments she had to deal with, it was nice to have one class she knew she would do well in. In a sense, every time she went to work she was studying for Anatomy.

* * *

The soft, winding strains of Chet Baker that filled Dr. Slikowski's office were interrupted by an abrupt knock at the door. Jenna jumped involuntarily, then caught her breath as the door swung open and Danny and Audrey walked in.

It was going on two-thirty, Friday afternoon, and for the last half hour or so, Jenna, Slick, and Dyson had been waiting in the M.E.'s office for the two Somerset detectives to show up. Danny had called en route to let them know that they had taken a bit longer than they'd intended interviewing a witness but were on their way.

Greetings were exchanged all around. Audrey sat down in the empty chair in the corner near Slick's CD player. Dyson was seated by the door while Jenna, feeling too nervous to sit still, leaned against the wall that held several of Slick's framed diplomas and awards. After closing the office door, Danny stood with his back against the wall, his arms folded across his chest.

"I appreciate that you could meet with us on such short notice, Walter," Audrey said.

"No problem whatsoever," Slick said quietly. He was sitting in his wheelchair behind his desk. "I only hope that we can be of some help."

Danny cleared his throat. "So do we. To be honest, we're a little baffled. Working with Boston P.D., we've checked out everything we could on incendiaries and other types of devices that could have been used to burn these two victims, but we still can't figure out how the killer did it."

Audrey shifted in her chair, took a long breath. Jenna saw how frustrated she looked and glanced at Danny, whom she realized was just as tired and overwhelmed as his partner.

"What can I do to help?" Slick asked with an earnest frown.

"We were hoping you'd be willing to reexamine the bodies, look for anything that could help us determine how they were burned," Audrey explained. "Not that we think you would have missed anything, of course."

"Of course," Slick said, waving the thought away with a slight smile. "Perish the thought."

As Audrey and Slick kept talking, Jenna looked over at Danny again. He was staring straight at her with his head cocked to one side, a look of concern on his face.

"From our research so far," Audrey went on, "it seems that in all of the incendiaries we checked, there should have been some traces of chemical residue on the victims or their clothing, or else some evidence of an external flame source. But nothing was found at the crime scenes or on the bodies during the autopsies you performed, and none of the witnesses saw anything of the kind."

Slick removed his glasses and lowered his head, thoughtfully rubbing the bridge of his nose. "The bodies haven't been remanded to the families for interment yet. They're still in the morgue, so it would be no problem to take another look at them. I'm just not exactly sure what we'd be looking for."

"Neither are we," Danny said, shaking his head. "But even if we can put together a motive on these killings, we still need to know how it was done to prove they were murdered. Anything would help."

Slick nodded. "My schedule happens to be clear for the rest of the afternoon and I don't mind working this evening if it will help your investigation. Dr. Dyson and I can get set up and begin work right away. Are you able to join us, Jenna?"

On the spot and feeling awkward, Jenna nodded. "I can be here if you need me."

"Terrific," Audrey said as she stood up and started for the door. "We'd appreciate any leads you can give us."

Danny opened the office door for Audrey, who exited first. He was about to follow her out, but he hesitated and turned back to Jenna. She smiled and followed him into the outer office.

"Hey," he said, keeping his voice low as she came closer to him.

Danny smiled and looked past her at Slick and Dyson, who were still in the M.E.'s private office. Neither of them seemed to be paying much attention, busy arranging for the new autopsies. At the door to the corridor, Audrey had slipped on her jacket and stood halfway into the corridor, looking back at Danny.

"You coming?" she called out.

Danny shot her a quick look and a nod, a silent communication that Audrey seemed to read perfectly. Without another word she went out, closing the door behind her.

"Why don't I walk you to the elevators?" Jenna asked.

"Okay."

Danny put his jacket on and Jenna opened the door and held it for him.

"You all right?" Danny asked. "You seem a little jumpy." His voice was almost a whisper, and he studied her with concern as he reached out and placed a gentle hand on her shoulder.

"I'm okay," she said. "How about you?"

Danny shrugged and ran his fingers through his hair.

"I'm doing okay," he said. "It's just . . . this case is tough, and I haven't been getting much sleep."

They walked together down the corridor and around the corner. Ahead, not far from the elevators, they could see Audrey.

"We should have lunch again soon," Jenna said, a bit cautiously. Her feelings for Danny were still there, but she had no idea what to do with them. All she did know was that, even if they were just friends, she wanted to spend more time with him.

"Yeah, definitely," Danny said with a quick nod. "This case is really eating up a lot of my time, but I could probably do dinner tomorrow, if that's good for you."

"Works for me."

"I'll give you a call in the morning so we can pick a place," he said. He seemed more than a little distracted, but Jenna knew—and understood—that it was just because the job was demanding his attention right now.

"Absolutely."

With a quick nod, Danny started down the hallway. The soles of his shoes clicked on the floor, echoing loudly from the tile walls. Jenna watched him get on the elevator with Audrey. Just before the doors closed, he gave her a wide smile and a wave. After a moment or two, she walked back to Slick's office, wondering what she was getting herself into. The last thing she needed was to set herself up for more hurt.

Friends. You're just friends, she told herself.

The orange flicker from the fireplace lit up the living room, making long, dark shadows dance against the walls. Outside, the northeast wind was blowing in powerful gusts off the ocean, slamming like invisible hammer blows against the back of the small house on the tip of Knowlton's Point on Cape Ann. Even through the closed windows, Matthew Dahms could hear the faint, steady ringing of the bell buoys in Rockport Harbor. Through the picture window, he could see the dark, tumultuous ocean and white-crested waves as they crashed against the rocky shore, sending spray high into the night air.

It was nearly midnight. Matthew's wife, Lois, had gone to bed more than two hours ago, but Matthew was still sitting in his armchair. The TV was off, and the book he had been reading was closed. He was doing nothing more than staring into the flames as he slowly sipped his brandy and let his mind wander.

Retirement is good, Matthew thought as a deep sense of satisfaction filled him.

Even in the depths of a New England winter, when the wind was so cold and raw it seemed to bite right through you, he seldom found himself wishing that he had moved to Florida like his brother, Eric. He liked the cold and the dark on the North Atlantic Ocean's edge, especially on a night like this when he could *feel* the weather changing and knew that another snowstorm was on the way. Spring had hinted at an early arrival. Now that seemed almost a cruel joke.

The firelight made the small house on Rowe Avenue feel even smaller and cozier than usual. The house had been built more than thirty years ago and had withstood more than its share of nor'easters. As long as they had plenty of food put aside, he didn't even care if they lost their electric power for a few days. Eating by candlelight was romantic.

Matthew sighed with satisfaction, feeling perfectly safe as he stared at the blazing logs in the fireplace and listened to the hollow whistle of the wind under the eaves. He had already started to doze off a little, even though he had not finished his customary nightcap, and was just thinking about retiring for the night when he heard something that didn't sound like it was just the wind slamming against the house.

Maybe the back door blew open, he thought as he turned and looked over his shoulder.

Could be one of the shutters is loose.

Matthew held his breath as he sat perfectly still for several seconds. He wanted to hear if the sound was repeated before he bothered to get up and investigate.

Might just have been something blowing across the yard, he thought.

He was just starting to ease down into his chair again when a chilly draft of air blew across the back of his neck, making him shiver. It only lasted for an instant, then it was gone. He dismissed it, attributing it to the fact that the rest of the house was getting colder because the thermostat on the living room wall was close to the fireplace. He was just starting to relax again when he heard what sounded like floorboards creaking in the kitchen.

With a grumble under his breath, he sat up, turned around, and stared into the kitchen.

There were no other lights in the house other than the glow from the fireplace, so all he could see was a dense wall of darkness. But as he stared into the kitchen, the darkness seemed to shift subtly, and Matthew thought he saw the shadowy outline of a person, standing motionless in the doorway. Thinking that he had to be imagining it, Matthew blinked a few times. But the figure remained.

Don't be ridiculous, he told himself as he shifted his weight forward and stood up. His left knee made a faint popping sound. *There can't be anyone else here.*

Keeping the chair between him and the kitchen doorway, Matthew leaned forward and tried to peer into the dense darkness. He found that if he looked a little to one side or the other, he could see the figure a bit better. It most definitely looked like there was someone standing in the doorway.

A ghost, maybe? He smiled in spite of the prickle of

fear at the back of his neck. A night like this, an old house at the edge of the ocean. A ghost almost seemed . . . appropriate.

"Are you . . . is someone there?" Matthew called out, his voice tight with tension.

All of his senses were focused on the doorway, and beneath the sound of the whistling wind outside, Matthew thought he heard a faint rumble of laughter from the darkness in the kitchen.

Am I going crazy? he wondered, suddenly fearful. *Am I hallucinating or what?*

But this was no hallucination.

The darkness in the doorway shifted and resolved. He could barely make out the silhouette of a man in the shadows.

"What the . . . ? What do you want here?" he asked, trying to suppress his rising fear and take control of the situation. "You know, I heard you breaking in and called nine-one-one. The police are already on their way."

"Your bluffs won't work with me," a low voice said from out of the darkness. It was deep and resonant, filled with menace.

Cold fear spiked through Matthew's chest. He heard his throat close off with an audible *click* and found it almost impossible to take a deep breath. His legs suddenly felt like they were going to collapse, so he leaned forward, bracing himself on the back of the armchair.

"I . . . I don't have any valuables, if that's what you're after," Matthew said. His chest and neck were aching with the rapid throb of his heart, and he felt unaccountably warm, even on his face, which was turned away from the fire.

"Please . . . just go," he pleaded.

The only answer was another deep rumble of laughter as the dark shape moved steadily toward him with outstretched hands.

Lois Dahms awoke to the sound of a loud, gargling scream. For a confused instant, she thought that she had been dreaming. She sat up and reached to snap on the lamp on her nightstand, and the sound came again—a raw, strangled scream that filled her with sudden dread.

"Matthew . . . ? Is that you, hon . . . ?" she called out.

Shivers danced up and down her back as she shifted her feet onto the floor, stood up, and took a few hesitant steps toward the bedroom doorway. Her body was tensed as she waited to hear if the sound repeated.

"Honey . . . ?"

She walked out into the hallway and looked down the stairway. The glow of flames from the fireplace seemed much brighter than she thought they should be, but she figured it was only that she had just woken up, and her eyes hadn't adjusted to the light.

"Matthew . . . ?" She started down the stairs.

When she was halfway down the sound came again. This time, although she was closer, it seemed much fainter.

It sounded like someone was choking.

Oh my God! No! she thought as she hurried down the rest of the stairs and entered the living room. At first, she thought that she must still be asleep and dreaming all of this. There was a rounded shape on the floor, engulfed by thick, oily orange flames that reached halfway up to the ceiling.

For one crazy instant, Lois tried to convince herself that the armchair Matthew had been sitting in had somehow caught fire. That was the burning shape on the floor.

But she was not asleep. Not dreaming. And the thing on the floor, the burning thing that stank so badly she had to cover her nose and mouth . . .

It wasn't a chair.

"Well, how about that?" the voice on the telephone said. "You know, it's not even six A.M. out here and it's already about eighty. Weatherman says it's gonna be a perfect day."

Danny was tapping the eraser end of a pencil on his desk blotter while talking to Sergeant Jose Gonzales of the Pasadena Police Department. He thought the man sounded maybe just a bit too smug about the California weather, but then he spun around in his chair and felt his spirits sink when he looked out his office window.

The storm had started overnight and even now, at going on nine o'clock, it looked like dawn had never actually arrived. Thick, soot-gray clouds swept low over the city as the blizzard rolled up the coast. Hopefully, this would be the last storm of the season, but there was already more than a foot of fresh snow on the ground, and the forecast was calling for at least another six inches before the blizzard finally stopped sometime in the late afternoon or early evening.

"You ever think about moving out here to Cali?" Gonzales asked cheerily.

Danny shook his head and sniffed with laughter. "Well, today I might consider it. So tell me, have you got anything on this guy Victor Frost?"

"You know, the man you should really talk to is Detective Hardy. Lawrence Hardy," Gonzales said. He sounded a little distracted, and Danny could hear the rapid-fire clicking of the man's keyboard as he scanned the department's computer files. "I'm running Frost's name now, but I seem to recall this guy was connected with something Hardy was working on a couple of years ago."

"But you don't remember exactly what it was?" Danny asked.

He knew he might be sounding a little too curt and edgy, but this case had really been getting to him, more than most. Two horribly burned murder victims were two too many, and he wanted to get to the bottom of it as fast as possible. It was fine that the M.E. had agreed to look at the victims again, and the Boston P.D. was still researching, and he and Audrey were interviewing known associates of the deceased, trying to figure out who might have had reason to want to do them in.

Danny, on the other hand, was also trying to see if Victor Frost fit into the Nash-Sobler scenario anywhere. Or at least finish up the background check so he could cross Frost's name off his things-to-do list.

"Nope. Sorry," Gonzales said. "I don't remember exactly. Hardy's in homicide, so it had to have been something to do with a murder, but as I recall, he wasn't involved directly in the investigation. I think Frost was living here in Pasadena at the time. The murder happened somewhere in L.A., I think."

"I'm guessing Hardy's not in the office now, right?" Danny said. He was still staring out the window at the curtain of snow, but he was too bothered by this case to see any beauty in the snowy day.

"No, he's not in 'til nine A.M. today. That'd be noon your time," Gonzales said. "Just my luck I get to work graveyard shift. Anyway . . . wait a second . . . yeah, here's something on Frost . . . hmm . . . yeah, now I remember."

"What have you got?" Danny asked, feeling a sudden rush of anticipation.

"Hang on," the California cop told him.

Although Danny appreciated the help Gonzales was giving him, he couldn't help but feel impatient at the delay. Of course, he could simply ask Gonzales to fax him whatever he had when he got it, but Danny wanted to get everything he could as soon as possible, so he bided his time, tapping his pencil on the palm of his hand while Gonzales scanned the files.

"Okay, there was a woman—Ellen Foster, from Santa Monica, who died. Burned to death at a nightclub . . . hmm . . ."

For several seconds, Gonzales was silent as he read more. Danny forced himself to stop tapping his pencil as he stared out at the blizzard and waited. The snow was so thick he could barely see the storefronts and businesses across the street.

The words hung in the air. *Burned to death.*

"Yeah . . . yeah. It's pretty freaky, all right," Gonzales said after a while. "This Foster woman was out clubbing with some friends. They were dancing at a place called Marseilles in Santa Monica, when apparently she burst into flames. That's what the witnesses said, anyway." Gonzales let out a loud gasp. "Man, this reads like science fiction or something. The report says the authorities couldn't determine the origin of the fire. And—yeah, here it is. I knew it. Victor Frost was one of the witnesses they interviewed, and they called Hardy for a background check. Frost wasn't a suspect or anything. Just on the scene at the time."

"When was this?" Danny asked, feeling an undeniable rush of excitement as he spun around to face his desk again. His pencil was poised above a sheet of paper, ready to take notes.

"Year before last. September twenty-seventh," Gonzales said, and Danny scribbled down the information.

"But they never figured out exactly what happened?" Danny asked. "What caused the fire in the first place?"

"Nope. Doesn't look that way."

"Would you fax that report to me?" Danny asked. "I'd like to take a closer look at it."

Danny was feeling almost giddy with anticipation as he gave Gonzales his fax number at the Somerset P.D.

Here was at least one apparent case of human spontaneous combustion in California, and Victor Frost had been present at the scene. Just like Alan Nash's death.

What are the odds of that? Danny wondered. Though he knew the answer. *Impossible.* Unless Frost was responsible.

"I'll get that right off to you," Gonzales said.

"Is there anything else you have on Victor Frost?" Danny asked. "DMV? Outstanding traffic tickets? Complaints from neighbors? Anything at all?"

"I'll have to search some other sources, but that's gonna take a little time," Gonzales said. "Look, why don't I read through all these reports and fax you whatever else I find, okay? It's six o'clock in the morning. Pretty slow right now. Shouldn't take very long."

"I'd really appreciate that," Danny said.

He glanced up when the office door opened. From the expression on Audrey's face, he knew she had something urgent to tell him. She walked over to his desk and stood there with her hands shoved into her pockets, waiting patiently for him to finish up his call. Danny raised his hand, signaling her that he was just about done.

"Thanks for your help. I'd appreciate it if you'd give Detective Hardy my telephone number," Danny said, "just in case he has anything more to add. That wouldn't be a problem, would it?"

"No. Not at all," Gonzales said cheerfully. "I'm glad I could help you out, Detective Marino."

"That's 'Mariano,' " Danny said. "I appreciate it."

He smiled to himself as he momentarily adopted a laid-back, California attitude and ended the conversation with a chipper, "You have yourself a nice day."

As he shifted forward in his chair to hang up the phone, Audrey moved a step closer. "We have to take a little drive today."

"In this weather?" Danny asked, scowling at her. He felt a sudden dropping sensation in his stomach. "Don't tell me there's been another one."

Audrey's expression remained totally impassive as she slowly nodded her head.

"Might be," she said grimly. "Guy up in Rockport, retired executive named Matthew Dahms, burned to death last night in his home."

"Oh, man," Danny said, closing his eyes and leaning his elbows on the edge of his desk. He started rubbing the sides of his head as though he had just gotten a sudden, intense migraine attack.

"Yeah," Audrey sighed. "It looks like the same M.O. We won't know for sure until we get there. Rockport says they'll cooperate fully. Said they'd never seen anything like this before."

Squinting, Danny looked up at her and smiled thinly.

"Yeah," he said as he slowly shifted his chair back and stood up. "And, unfortunately, we have."

The weatherman had predicted eight inches of snow, but that was before the storm had slowed, then stalled, right above eastern Massachusetts. The streets around campus had rumbled all night long with the sound of passing snowplows and sanding trucks, but the snow just kept on coming, filling in behind them. The drifts were already huge, and growing. Like the song said, it showed no sign of stopping.

"Wow! It's a winter wonderland," Jenna said, feeling a rush of exhilaration as she looked out her dorm window at the fresh blanket of white. Ever since she was little, she had always enjoyed a good snowstorm. It made everything so clean and white. Jenna watched the storm through her window. The flakes were fat and wet and piled up quickly. She felt nine years old again.

"Hey, want to go traying on the library hill?"

"Umm . . . we could do that," Yoshiko muttered sleepily from the top bunk. "Or maybe we could catch up on our sleep because we were up so late studying last night."

"Is *that* what you and Hunter call it? *Studying?*" Jenna asked with a snicker. " 'Cause that's a euphemism I've never heard before."

Yoshiko let out a loud, exasperated groan as she rolled over onto her side with her back to Jenna. She pulled her pillow over her head.

"Sorry," Jenna said. "But there's all this beautiful snow, I can't help but be happy."

"Hooray for you," Yoshiko replied sleepily, her voice almost completely muffled by the pillow.

Jenna laughed softly at her roommate's exhausted teasing and looked back out at the late winter snow. It really was beautiful. Even better, though, was thinking about how she was going to get together with Danny later. He hadn't called her yet to arrange the exact time and place where they would meet. He was probably too busy. She was a bit worried that the snow would put a crimp in their plans.

Realizing that her roomie wasn't in nearly as good a mood as she was, Jenna decided to head down to the showers and then hit an early breakfast, alone. She thought about giving Roseanne a call to see if she wanted to go traying on the hill, but before she could do that, the telephone rang.

That's probably Roseanne now, calling with the same idea, she thought. She picked up the phone quickly so it wouldn't ring again and disturb Yoshiko.

"Good morning," she said, with a merry, cavalier note in her voice. Even as she spoke she glanced up at the top bunk to see that Yoshiko had fallen back to sleep.

"Jenna?"

She recognized Dr. Slikowski's voice immediately and knew before he said anything else that something had happened.

"I'm sorry to be calling you so early," Slick said, "but something's come up, and I need your help later today, if you're available."

"Sure thing," Jenna said, her voice just above a whisper. "What is it?"

"There's been an immolation case up in Rockport that's apparently similar to the ones we've had locally," Slick said. "The Essex County M.E. has agreed to let me examine the body, and since Dyson's not available, I thought you might like to come along."

"Yes. Absolutely," Jenna said quickly. "When do you want me?"

"The M.E.'s lab is at Danvers Hospital, which is usually only half an hour from here," Slick said. "With the snow and all, it might take us a bit longer. How about if I pick you up in front of Sparrow Hall at eleven o'clock?"

"Sure. That'd be perfect," Jenna said.

This meant that she would have to skip breakfast and do some studying for her European history test next Wednesday. She'd been so occupied with Spanish and Shakespeare that she'd been putting it off, but now the test was only four days away. Still, if she started now, and studied a little each day, she thought she could still be ready in time for the test.

Traying was obviously out. Instead of fun, cutting up another torched cadaver. *Yay!*

So much for my winter wonderland.

Yet somehow she was not as disappointed as she might have been. This case had started off just bizarre and disgusting, but it was quickly becoming a fascinating puzzle. Jenna had always loved a good puzzle.

"I'll see you at eleven," she told Slick, and they both hung up.

"Oh, boy . . . Danny," she whispered, suddenly realizing that if she left with Slick at eleven o'clock, depending how the day went, she might not be back from Danvers in time to meet him. She quickly dialed Danny's number at work. After three rings, his voice mail picked up.

"Hi, Danny. It's me. You probably already heard

about the incident in Rockport. Slick wants me to go with him to the Essex County M.E.'s and help examine the body, so I may not be back in time for dinner tonight. I'll call you as soon as I get back, and we'll see what's what. 'Kay? Bye."

After she hung up, she looked up to see that Yoshiko was still sound asleep. Jenna tried to study but could not seem to focus. Her mind was occupied with the challenge this new mystery presented. Someone was using fire to kill. How they were doing it was a big question mark. But now that there had been a third one, there seemed little doubt there would be even more unless they could figure out the who and how and why and the police could stop him.

The clock was ticking.

"The burns aren't quite as bad as they could have been," said Dr. John Halmen, assistant to the Essex County M.E. "The victim's wife reacted fast, trying to smother the flames by wrapping him up in a throw rug. Of course, it wasn't fast enough to save his life, but it did extinguish the flames. Still, you can see what look like scorch marks on the flesh, indicating the direction the flames took as they swept over him."

"Or around him, more likely," Slick said.

Like Jenna, he was wearing a green surgical mask and gown. He leaned forward and carefully studied the charred remains of Matthew Dahms. The autopsy table wasn't specially designed, as Slick's was, to accommodate his wheelchair, so he had to strain to get close enough to examine the victim.

The lingering smell of burned hair and human flesh in the room made Jenna's stomach churn, but she also moved closer to the body to get a better view. She tried to avoid looking directly into the black holes of the victim's vacant eye sockets. It was easy enough to distance herself from the process of examining what, just a day ago, had been a living, breathing human being unless she looked at where the eyes used to be.

"The report says that he had a fire going in the fireplace," Slick said. "Are they absolutely certain that this wasn't caused by a spark flying out and setting his clothes on fire?"

"The investigators have ruled that out," Dr. Halmen said. "The fire screen was securely closed, and there was no evidence that the fire could have originated there. They also found that the back door had been broken open, and there was other evidence of forced entry. Also, the flames spread too quickly to have been accidental. I mean . . . look at him. It had to have happened fast. And his wife got to him fast enough that nothing else in the house was burned except for a spot on the carpet."

Jenna was surprised to hear the hesitation and horror in Dr. Halmen's voice. He was at least forty years old and had likely been at his job long enough to have seen some pretty horrifying stuff. Then again, she hoped she never got used to it herself. Not ever.

"Just covering all the bases," Slick said.

He leaned forward and, using a pair of forceps, started picking at the black flakes of skin at the base of the victim's neck. Jenna noticed that they seemed almost to overlap, like shingles on a house.

"You know what it looks like?" she said.

Slick grunted but didn't turn away from his close examination of the body.

"Melted candle wax," Jenna said. "It looks like, as he was burning, his skin . . . melted . . ." Her stomach did a little flip. "Like it slid down his neck, overlapping burned flesh."

"You're absolutely right," Slick said, casting an appreciative glance at her. "And look here, on the temporal lobe." He indicated the left side of the victim's head, just above the curled, burned remains of his ear. "What does that look like to you?"

Jenna moved even closer to the body and studied the side of the dead man's head for a full thirty seconds before answering.

"It's darker than the rest of the burns," she finally said. "It could be where the fire started." She was surprised and privately pleased with herself that she could detect the pattern in the blackened flesh.

"That's what it looks like to me, too," Slick said. "Look at how the scorch marks radiate outward from here. You can see how it looks almost like an impact crater. Everything radiates outward from this darker central point, as if the flames originated there. It doesn't make any sense, of course—the fire would have had to almost, well, erupt there and then spread instantaneously over the rest of his body—but that is what it looks like."

Once again Slick glanced over his shoulder at

Jenna. She could see the corners of his eyes crinkle as he smiled at her.

"You've got a good eye for detail, Jenna," he said with a strong note of pride in his voice.

Jenna was still concentrating on the burn marks, trying to imagine what had happened.

"It's almost like something, the source of the fire, struck him on the side of the head, and then he—"

"Went up," Slick finished for her.

"But how?" Jenna asked. "They didn't find any traces of chemicals on the body. How could it spread that fast naturally?"

"My point exactly," Slick replied. "And if this case is connected with the other two, Nash and Sobler, why didn't we see a similar pattern somewhere on their remains?"

Jenna could not stop staring. Her mind was working fast, and she was barely listening to Slick now. He turned his wheelchair toward her just a bit, looking at her with concern in his eyes.

"What?" he asked, his voice low, restrained.

"No, it . . . it's impossible," she said, shaking her head.

"Apparently it isn't, for here it is," Slick told her, indicating the corpse on the table. "So what could have done it? If we've ruled out chemicals or sparks from the fireplace, what started it? Look closely here. Do you see?"

Using the tip of his forceps, Slick indicated a wide, irregular black splotch on the side of the victim's head where the flesh was burned to a crisp.

"It wasn't a pinpoint, like from a spark or an electrical igniter, where the flames started. It looks more like—"

"My God! It looks like a handprint!" Jenna said, astonished.

For a moment she thought her eyes must be playing tricks on her and that she was imagining seeing the pattern in the charred flesh the same way, as a child, she used to make out figures and designs in the clouds. But even when she looked at it carefully, the scorch mark looked vaguely like the palm of a hand above the ear, with four long, narrow marks reaching like fingers around the back of the head.

"That can't just be a coincidence," Jenna said, shaking her head in amazement.

When Slick did not respond right away, she knew that he was still considering the possibilities. Without a word, he propelled his wheelchair around to the other side of the table. Straining to lean forward, he pulled himself up as close as he could to the body so he could see the right side of the victim's head. After a moment, he let out a soft, satisfied grunt and pointed to a similar scorch mark just above the corpse's right ear.

"It may not be coincidental at all," Slick finally said as he pushed his wheelchair away from the autopsy table. "Imagine that the killer confronted the victim, grabbed him by the sides of the head with both hands, and held him like that as he burst into flames."

Dr. Halmen cleared his throat. "How would the killer have kept himself from being burned?"

Jenna looked closely at Slick's eyes and saw there a reflection of her own bewilderment. A thought had been running through her mind ever since she had noticed the handprints. She almost did not dare to put voice to it but impossible as it was, it fit.

"What about pyrokinesis?"

"Oh, come on," Dr. Halmen interjected. "You must be joking."

The lower half of Halmen's face was covered by a green surgical mask, but Jenna had the distinct impression that, behind his mask, he might be laughing at both of them.

Slick frowned at her. "Jenna? Not that I want to discourage intuitive thinking or exploration of ideas some would consider outrageous, but . . ."

His words trailed off. Apparently the M.E. was not sure how to continue.

Sheepish, Jenna shrugged. "You were willing to consider spontaneous human combustion as an explanation before."

"I'm not sure I believe in spontaneous human combustion," Slick replied. "But, no matter how dubious, there are numerous documented cases. It was something to at least consider."

Dr. Halmen scoffed. "For you, maybe."

"Is this really that much further a leap?" Jenna continued. "I did a paper in high school on research done on all that stuff back when Russia was still the Soviet Union. Telepathy. Telekinesis. Clairvoyance. And pyrokinesis."

"Cold war hyperbole," Halmen said almost angrily.

He glared at Slick. "You can't possibly believe any of this?"

Slick, obviously offended, shot Halmen a withering glance from his wheelchair. "I may not believe it, but I'm not so rude as to deny her the right to think."

That shut the other doctor up. Jenna was glad. It was all she could do not to smile at the man's sudden discomfort.

"There are documented cases," Jenna forged ahead. "Just like with spontaneous combustion."

"Though from what little I've read I believe the sources for the documentation regarding pyrokinesis and in general the power of the mind are more suspect. We were in a cold war with the Soviets at that time. It was beneficial to them to have us believe they had people who could do such things."

"Those aren't the only cases," Jenna argued. Then she smiled and shook her head, feeling awkward. "Sorry. I don't mean to go on about it, and I'm not even saying I believe it. It's just that this whole puzzle, all these little mysteries, they're all questions with no answers. Let's face it, we have a total—and I mean total—absence of any source for the fire. No accelerants of any kind. Now these handprints. Crazy as it sounds, pyrokinesis is the one answer that makes all the puzzle pieces fit together."

Slick stroked his chin thoughtfully, bent forward in his chair. After a moment, he glanced up at Jenna, ignoring Halmen completely. "If spontaneous human combustion is a real phenomenon—and don't forget that I said 'if'—it would require the buildup of a great deal of heat and energy inside the human body. I suppose that it follows that if the one is possible, it is not really that far a leap to consider that a human being might be able to induce that buildup of energy internally and then discharge that same energy as heat. Or flame. All of it sounds a great deal like science fiction, however."

"Maybe," Jenna agreed, and shrugged. "And maybe it's time we did some research of our own."

"I suspect we'll be wasting time that could be better spent on more traditional investigation. There is no evidence to suggest pyrokinesis actually exists," Slick told her doubtfully. "On the other hand, I won't have it said that I don't have an open mind. We might as well look into it."

"I think you two have been whiffing the formaldehyde a little too much," Halmen said with a scowl. "And you're going to have a lot of people laughing at you. Do me a favor, if you mention any of this cockamamy theory to anyone? Leave me out of it, okay?"

"Gladly," Slick replied, totally unfazed by the other doctor's reaction.

Jenna had to admire Slick for being so cool in the face of what bordered on professional ridicule. Still, something bothered her about all of this.

"Hold on a second," she said, trying to clear her mind and think it all through. "You were bothered because we didn't see any marks like these on the other two victims. Maybe that's because he didn't touch their skin. He was in a crowd both times. It would have been too conspicuous to try to touch their faces or necks . . . okay, hands maybe, but go with it a second. Maybe the reason we didn't find the same kind of burn marks on them is that he only touched their clothes."

Slick removed his surgical mask slowly, obviously lost in thought.

"At the very least, we ought to have a look at their clothes," he finally said with a slow, pensive nod. "Though I'm reluctant to share this line of investigation with Detectives Gaines and Mariano, I think we must. An examination of Nash's and Sobler's clothing might enlighten us further."

Since the death of her husband, Lois Dahms had moved in with her sister, Helen Pistenmaa, at her house in Lanesville. When Danny and Audrey arrived at the Pistenmaa residence, Lois greeted them at the door with dark bags under her red-rimmed eyes. The woman had obviously been crying a great deal, and she looked unsteady on her feet as she stepped back to allow the detectives to enter. Her sister nodded a silent greeting from where she stood, watching quietly from the kitchen doorway.

"We want to thank you for agreeing to speak with us so soon after your tragic loss, Mrs. Dahms," Audrey said, nodding sympathetically as the elderly woman led them into the living room.

"Please, make yourselves comfortable," Lois said in a shaky voice. "Could I get either of you a glass of water, or some coffee, perhaps?"

"No, thank you. We're fine," Danny said, keeping

his voice low and respectful. "We just want to clear up a few questions, and then we'll be on our way."

Danny waited until Lois and Audrey had taken a seat before sitting down in a comfortable armchair and flipping open his notebook. Helen remained standing in the kitchen doorway. Danny cleared his throat, finding it difficult to begin. It was always tough, asking questions of the survivors, especially so soon after the tragedy, but it had to be done.

"We're investigating some recent deaths in the Boston area," he began, "and they appear to be somewhat similar to what happened to your husband last night. You've probably already answered all these questions for the Rockport police, so I apologize for going over them again. It's only that we may find different angles to pursue. First off, what did your husband do for work?"

"Oh, he was retired," Lois replied in a frail voice. "But up until a year ago, he owned and operated the Mercury Courier Service. The main office was in Boston, but there were branches all over the North Shore. He just sold the business last year, and we were thinking about moving down to Florida. I wanted to, anyway. He wasn't so keen on the idea."

Just mentioning their plans that now would never happen brought fresh tears to Lois's eyes. She drew a tissue from the pocket of her baggy sweater and dabbed them away before they could fall.

"I know this might be a difficult question to answer," Danny said, folding his hands and leaning forward with a sympathetic look, "but is there anyone you can think of who might have been angry at your husband for some reason? A business associate or a neighbor who might have wanted to harm your husband?"

"No. Absolutely not," Lois replied. Danny detected a note of irritation or hurt in her voice that he would even suggest such a thing. "Everyone loved my Matthew. He was a wonderful man. He didn't have an enemy in the world!"

"What about a man named Alan Nash?" Danny asked. He could see how painful this was for her, and he wanted to get the interrogation over with as quickly as possible. "Did you or your husband ever know a man by that name?"

For a moment Lois's eyes went unfocused as more tears gathered. Looking past Danny, she pursed her thin, pale lips into a tight line as she thought for a moment, then shook her head slightly.

"No," she said, her voice not much more than a breathy whisper. "I—I'm sorry, but I don't recall that name."

"How about Kendall Sobler?" Danny said. "That's a woman's name, by the way."

Again, Lois stared blankly ahead for a few seconds before replying.

"No. Sorry. That name doesn't ring a bell, either."

"How about a man named Frost . . . Victor Frost?" Danny asked. He tensed as he asked the question, expecting to wait while Mrs. Dahms ran through her memory, but she surprised him by answering quickly.

"Oh, heavens, yes. Of course I know Vic."

Danny inhaled sharply.

"He worked for Matthew off and on for four or five years, though he took a year or so off when he moved out to California. He was one of our very best drivers. We even had him over to the house a few times for supper. He was always trustworthy and prompt. I remember Matthew saying so. That's why he rehired Vic when he came back from California."

Bingo! Danny thought, feeling grim satisfaction as he and Audrey exchanged glances. Nodding sympathetically, he closed his notebook and slipped it into his coat pocket as he and Audrey stood up in unison.

"We won't take any more of your time, Mrs. Dahms," he said softly as he zipped up his coat, preparing to step out into the cold. "I want to thank you. You've been a tremendous help."

Lois rose shakily from the couch and walked them to the door.

"You'll find him, won't you?" she said. Her voice cracked with restrained emotion and near desperation. "You'll find the person who killed my Matthew, won't you?"

Danny and Audrey looked at her, and both of them nodded solemnly.

"We're doing everything we can, Mrs. Dahms," Audrey said softly but firmly. "I promise you that."

chapter 8

Danny's eyes burned.

He had the car window down all the way, letting the cold wind and random dusting of snow blow into his face as he drove to City Hall. It was Sunday morning, but the heavy gray sky gave no evidence that a new day had dawned. If anything, it was colder than the day before and though the snowstorm had passed, the weather patterns meant squalls and flurries swirled through the area at unpredictable intervals. The city had done a less than stellar job of clearing the snow initially. Danny figured they expected it to burn off in a couple of days, it being so late in the winter. But the weather gave no signs of surrendering to a sudden warming trend.

He was exhausted.

The events of the previous day—and night—flashed through his mind incessantly as he tried to make sense of it all. Of course, after Lois Dahms had confirmed Victor Frost as an ex-employee, and after the M.E. had suggested a radical possibility as to the method of the murders . . . it had been a very long night. Along with Audrey, Danny had made a new round of phone calls about Victor Frost, establishing other employers, checking nationally for prior arrests, looking for known associates in California and Massachusetts.

The guy was like a ghost. Nobody knew him. Maybe nobody *wanted* to know him. It was a long night spent pretty fruitlessly, partially because it was a Saturday. Most people had made themselves scarce for the weekend. Most people didn't have a series of burning homicides to contend with. Now it was Sunday, and he didn't think things were going to shake loose much before tomorrow morning.

Guess that depends how hard I shake the tree, he thought.

Danny rubbed at his eyes, leaned his head a little out the window to catch the full blast of the cold wind. He had fallen asleep after three in the morning with the TV still on and awoken at six-thirty with infomercials yapping at him from the screen. Hiss and static would have been a more pleasurable way to meet the day, but the world had cable twenty-four hours a day now, not like when he was a kid. No "Star-Spangled Banner" before sign-off. The broadcast day never ended.

Neither did the investigative day, when he was up to his eyeballs in a homicide case.

With a sigh, he changed the radio station, clicking

over to a modern rock station. He'd been listening to WEEI newsradio all morning to see if the press had connected the dots yet, and he was grateful that they had not. All they needed to screw up the investigation now was a bunch of cranks confessing to the murders.

Alan Nash. Kendall Sobler. Matthew Dahms.

At the moment the only thing that connected all three was the manner of their demise. Hall Boggs and his crew at Boston P.D. were running down known arsonists, but that was just to cover all the bases. But given what he'd learned from the California cops, Danny was now convinced Victor Frost would be at the center of the web that strung the murders together. *Just got to find the right angle,* he told himself.

And be careful. Those had been the last words in the message Jenna left on his voice mail the previous afternoon.

By the time Jenna had called, he had already figured their plans had been nixed by Dahms's murder. Audrey had spoken to Slick. The M.E. made it a habit not to make any statement he was not sure was one hundred percent true. In this case, though, he told Audrey he felt a responsibility to let them know about the handprints on Dahms's throat and neck, the scorch marks, and about his conversation with Jenna about pyrokinesis, which both detectives thought was just about the wildest hypothesis the man had ever had. Even Slick didn't seem to believe in it, but he brought it up just the same.

Jenna's message. *Be careful.*

Danny's response to Audrey when she informed him of Slick's cautious suggestion. *You've gotta be kidding me.* He was thinking exactly the same thing now as he steered his way warily through the remains of Friday night's blizzard. Problem was, he had racked his brain to come up with an alternative to Slick's wild implication, and he'd found no evidence to support any other theory.

There has to be something, he thought as he guided his battered vehicle into the parking lot in front of City Hall. *Some kind of incendiary we haven't come up with yet. Has to be.*

The alternative was just too much. In his years as a cop, Danny had seen bizarre and worse. But for some reason, he had a particularly hard time with this one.

It's too much power, he suddenly realized. *That's what's got you so creeped out at the idea. Psychoactive chemicals and rare skin disorders are one thing, but setting fires with a touch, just using the power of your mind, that's too much. Too dangerous.*

A picture of Victor Frost sneaked into Danny's thoughts again, eyes slitted, sitting in the interview room with a cigarette clenched between his teeth and looking cocky as hell. Danny shuddered.

He killed the ignition on his Cutlass—he'd bought it used the previous month, got a great deal because of the dented left front quarter panel, and loved it for its sixteen-valve engine and the way the inside felt like a cockpit. The radio snapped off with the engine.

Danny slid out from behind the wheel, locked the door, and headed for the front steps.

He was halfway across the lot when an image flashed in his head.

Danny frowned and turned around. When he had pulled into the lot, he had noticed a pair of State Police cruisers in his peripheral vision, but he had been so preoccupied that their presence had barely registered. Now it did.

On his way up the stairs to the homicide squad room, he muttered under his breath, mostly out of frustration with himself. *Stupid,* he thought. A murder in Rockport meant Essex County—the killer had crossed county lines. That made it a state case, no question. He had known it, of course, but had been so wrapped up in the investigation that he had not taken the time to consider the implications.

Sure enough, when he entered the squad, it was a full house. Eight-thirty on a Sunday morning, and there were more cops in the room than at most crime scenes. Three uniformed state troopers—two male, one female—stood in a clutch by the door to the break room. A pair of graying Staties in plainclothes huddled behind the glass in Lieutenant Gonci's office with Gonci and Hall Boggs. A couple of detectives Danny recognized as part of Boston Homicide were crowded around Audrey's desk with two men he'd never seen before but assumed were from Rockport P.D. As Danny walked into the room, they all glanced at him.

Audrey motioned him over from the midst of that group.

"Dunkin' Donuts have to close? Or are we having a charity cookout, and no one told me?" he asked his partner as he joined them.

There were a few chuckles. Also a few wary glances at the state troopers. Danny felt as if he were in junior high again, trying to cadge a cigarette on the playground in front of the recess monitors. He had smoked for about a month when he was twelve—and only inhaled once. Cigarettes made him sick. Sticking burning weeds in his mouth had lost its appeal pretty fast.

"Do they talk?" he asked.

Audrey smiled. "You're in a good mood this morning."

"Nah. Just high on life."

Introductions were made all around. The Rockport detectives were Faber and Reichert. Lieutenant Boggs's team were Aaron Simms and Lisa Eckhardt. Danny got a decent vibe off all of them, though he thought Faber had a bit too much caveman in his blood. Not that there was anything standoffish about the guy, but he had broad shoulders and big fists with scarred knuckles, and something about him just screamed *thug,* as if he were the kind of cop to whom a perp's constitutional rights stopped outside the interrogation room.

Don't judge a book by its cover. That was what he'd been taught all his life. But as a homicide detective, it was his job to make snap judgments. He'd keep an eye on Faber if the guy was in the field with them.

"What's the story?" Danny asked Audrey, his voice hushed.

With a glance at the others, she turned slightly to exclude them without being extraordinarily rude, and they took the hint, giving the Somerset detectives some space. It was Danny and Audrey's home turf, after all.

"Pretty much what it looks like," Audrey whispered. "State's taking over. At least officially. The tall guy, he's in charge. A captain. Wessell, I think his name is. He made some noise about just coordinating the various departments. Gonci and Boggs are hashing that out at the moment."

"Or they were," Danny muttered, glancing over Audrey's shoulder.

She turned to see the four senior officers emerge from Gonci's office. They all looked pretty stiff. Danny watched them, wondering if he would ever really want to command a detective squad if it meant he had to look that uptight.

The tall guy Audrey had mentioned was easily six six, maybe two hundred. Lanky for his height. He wore glasses and had somehow managed, despite his height, to avoid looking like Frankenstein's monster. To Danny's mind, most guys that big tended to look unnatural. Not Wessell. Particularly not standing next to Lieutenant Boggs, a mountain of a man.

Gonci glanced at Wessell. The state police captain shrugged.

"Your house, your show, Lieutenant," Wessell told him.

"Obliged," Gonci replied, then cleared his throat. He had the attention of the room, even the silent troopers. "We'll make this quick because we want this case run down before the press gets wind of what's really happening here."

Do you know what's really happening here? Danny thought. *'Cause I sure don't.*

"Captain Wessell is going to be working out of an office at Boston Homicide for the duration of this investigation. Given that we're all already working this case, he's agreed the best course of action is for that to continue. So until further notice, Captain Wessell is running the Nash, Sobler, and Dahms investigations. Chief Martens in Rockport, Lieutenant Boggs, and I will all submit regular reports to Captain Wessell. You will all continue to report to your usual superior officers, but a joint task force is formed as of this moment, comprising the detectives in this room.

"Detective Gaines, you'll join Lieutenant Boggs's team and work on the Nash-Sobler relationship and known associates. See if we can get a connection to Victor Frost in there, but let's not marry ourselves so tightly to him as a suspect that we miss other possibilities.

"Mariano, you'll head up to Rockport this morning with detectives Reichert and Faber. We agree Victor Frost may be our man. Fine. Let's get something more than circumstantial evidence. You've got him connected to Matthew Dahms. Mrs. Dahms has graciously agreed to allow us to go through all the records from her husband's business pertaining to the years Mercury Courier employed Victor Frost. Find a connection to Nash or Sobler."

Danny shot a quick glance at Faber who was watching him with curiosity. He hoped the man wasn't the Neanderthal he appeared to be.

"Captain Wessell?" Gonci said, deferring to the other man.

"Just a couple of other things," Wessell said. "Boston P.D.'s got a tail on Frost now. Lieutenant Boggs promises me their best surveillance man is running that show."

A lot of the detectives in the room glanced inquisitively at Boggs. The lieutenant nodded.

"Jace Castillo," he said.

There were murmurs of assent all around. Danny knew Castillo from a particularly ugly case a few months back—a case that almost cost the man his career and then his life. It was good to know he was back up to speed on the job.

"You should also know that state police detectives are using every connection, scouring every resource for information on chemical or mechanical devices that might have been used as a weapon by the killer to create these fires," Wessell said.

Danny wondered what Wessell would think if he heard Slick and Jenna's theory on that subject. He certainly was not going to be the one to bring it up.

Wessell rubbed his hands together vigorously.

"Now go get the job done."

Faber smoked too much. Ate pretty much constantly, and nothing good for him. Reichert razzed him about his suspect interview skills, which were about what Danny expected—direct intimidation and nothing more. But beyond that, he turned out to be an amiable cop with more brain than he probably got credit for.

Rockport was a beautiful town, even covered in snow. Maybe more so, though it was best known as a seaside summer tourist hot spot. The town held a bonfire on Back Beach every Fourth of July, and Danny thought it was ironic that the Dahms's back porch had a view across the bay of the very spot where that fire blazed each year. Too many grim thoughts, too much gruesome humor in his head.

The basement of the Dahms family home was enormous. The available space was almost nil. Boxes of old records dating back to the mid-seventies were stacked high all around. Matthew Dahms apparently never threw anything away, and despite the fact that it boded well for their search for information, Danny could not help but dread exploring all those boxes.

Lois Dahms was kind enough to give over her dining room to the detectives. Boxes were stacked in the corners, files spread across the massive mahogany table. The huge windows rattled under gusts of chill air, and the sky outside was still a dark, ominous gray; at least the sight of the white-capped waves far out on the ocean gave them something to look at when their eyes started to cross from scanning so many files.

Behind the wheel of his Cutlass, Danny had followed Faber and Reichert back up to Rockport and to the Dahmses' residence. They had hit the basement and started lugging boxes up at just after ten o'clock in the morning.

Eight hours ago.

"Eric, it's after six. I should at least run out for sandwiches or something, don't you think?" Faber asked, with a pleading glance at his partner.

Reichert sighed. "You've been eating all day, Norman."

Faber grumbled and swore at Reichert good-naturedly, then turned to Danny for support. "You've gotta be hungry, Mariano. Tell 'im, will you?"

The truth was, Danny had been so wrapped up in work that he had not thought about food since Faber had come back with pizza just after one. He knew he should eat, but he was not hungry. On the other hand, Faber's expression was just so pitiful.

"Yeah, I could use a bite to eat," Danny admitted.

Faber threw his hands up.

"All right. Go," Reichert said, eyes going quickly back to the file in front of him.

Danny returned his attention to the delivery receipts in front of him. It all would have been much easier if Mercury Courier had kept an overall client database. They had one now, but it had only been started in the previous eighteen months, once the new owner had taken over.

He turned over a few more receipts as Faber pulled his thick winter coat on. It occurred to him that he should pick up the dinner tab since the Rockport boys paid for lunch. He pulled out his wallet and peeled two twenties out of his billfold, leaving a ten and a lonely trio of ones. *Lucky Thirteen*. The other detectives mumbled their thanks.

Nodding, Danny began to flip the next receipt over, working his way through the stack.

He paused, put it down and stared at it again.

"Jesus," he whispered.

"What?" Reichert snapped.

Faber stood in the arched entrance to the dining room. "You got something?"

Mouth hanging slightly open, Danny glanced up at them and nodded slowly. "I've got exactly what we're looking for. Never thought we'd find it in this mess, but . . ." He held up the delivery receipt. "Three years ago. Artwork delivered from Tech-Style Design to Cragmore Advertising. Victor Frost was the courier. Kendall Sobler was the receptionist at Cragmore. Look here. She signed for the package."

"Holy Christ," Faber muttered. "That's it."

Danny stood up, paced a bit. "So Frost delivers to Cragmore. Meets Sobler. Maybe falls for her? Maybe he asks her out; maybe he doesn't. Either way, he has a thing for her, so he keeps an eye on her, even after he's not working for Mercury anymore. When he finds out Sobler's seeing this guy Nash . . ."

"Uh-huh. It fits," Faber agreed quickly.

"It does, but we need more," Reichert cautioned, though his eyes shone with his own excitement over the find. "One won't be enough to make that story fly. We need a bunch of those receipts, establish a paper trail, and we need a warm body to put Frost and Sobler together."

"We'll find them," Danny said. He sat back down and started moving much more quickly through the stack of receipts there.

Faber took off his jacket.

None of them said another word about dinner until almost eleven at night. By then, they had seventeen receipts connecting Victor Frost to Kendall Sobler.

By Monday morning Audrey was already tired of working with the two Boston detectives and wishing she had Danny covering her back. All right, Lieutenant Boggs and Jace Castillo were stand-up, solid cops. She supposed there was nothing wrong with Eckhardt and Simms, either, the two she was saddled with, but they seemed a bit too arrogant about the fact that they were Boston's Finest, and she was on the job in Somerset. Like Somerset was some dusty backwater that never saw any kind of action instead of the satellite city it was.

Audrey was tempted to get up in Simms's face, get the peacock to go case for case with her, see whose track record really measured up. But she knew that was foolish thinking. Nothing she could say would change his attitude, and the case was much more important.

The case.

It brought a smile to her face every time she thought of the fact that it was Danny, along with a pair of detectives from a seaside suburb, who tagged the biggest lead so far. No doubt it burned Simms's backside, probably Eckhardt's, too, though the woman didn't seem quite as pompous as her partner.

Go, Danny-boy, Audrey thought.

"What's so funny?" Simms asked, a deep frown creasing his forehead.

"Private joke," Audrey told him, barely polite.

Eckhardt smiled at her, and Audrey wondered if she shouldn't revise her opinion of the other woman. Lisa Eckhardt apparently enjoyed seeing her partner get a bit of a spanking. Maybe she wasn't so bad after all.

They stood in the conference room at Cragmore Advertising. The executive board had grudgingly allowed them to set up camp to interview employees throughout the day. *Grudgingly*, Audrey thought. *A woman in their employ is fried on the sidewalk, and the only reason they cooperate is 'cause of how it would look if they didn't.*

There was a knock on the door to the conference room.

"Come," Simms commanded.

Audrey didn't even have the energy to roll her eyes at his imperious tone. His arrogance had tired her out. In the presence of Lieutenant Boggs, he stifled it. Out of sight, he acted like the chief of police.

The door opened, and Elena Manoff poked her head in. Her eyes betrayed her nervousness, but when she saw Audrey, she visibly relaxed. Audrey stood up, a warm smile on her face, and walked toward the woman.

"Elena," she said. "Thanks for agreeing to talk to me again."

Simms grunted, perturbed that his role was being usurped. "Yes, your cooperation is appreciated, Miss . . ."

Audrey smiled at him, one eyebrow raised. "Manoff. Elena Manoff. She was close to the deceased and was instrumental in providing the link between Miss Sobler and Alan Nash."

"Excellent, yes," Simms said, peering down his nose at both of them. "Please have a seat, Miss Malov."

"Manoff," Elena corrected.

Her eyes were sad as she slid into one of the comfortable leather chairs around the long table, chairs usually reserved for members of the company's executive board and clients. Elena seemed uncomfortable, but Audrey was unsure whether her awkwardness came from her surroundings or just from being in the room with Simms.

The man bulldozed his way through a preliminary interview that covered only things Audrey had already asked Elena Manoff days earlier. Several times, she shot comforting glances Elena's way, but they did not seem to help. Simms behaved like his questioning techniques came from a fifties cop show.

When he took a breath, Lisa Eckhardt broke in. "Miss Manoff, do you know of any other men Kendall dated?"

Elena thought a moment, then shook her head. "She went on dates here and there. Over the years I've known her—knew her, I'd guess she went out with a dozen different guys, at least. But usually it was just one or two dates, and then just nothing, y'know?" She glanced at Audrey. "That's the way it goes."

Audrey nodded. She knew.

"Alan was different. Her knight in shining armor. That's what Kendall called him. Until she found out he was seeing someone else, this Laura Depuy. Apparently Alan had gone out with her before he met Kendall and they'd been getting back together. Kendall told him to hit the road." Elena bit her lower lip, and her eyes grew moist. "Even so, when Alan was killed she . . ."

The woman broke off, wiped at her eyes.

"Have you ever heard the name Victor Frost?" Simms asked bluntly.

Elena considered, then shook her head. "Doesn't ring a bell." She looked up, suddenly aware, frowning. "Is that the man who did all this?"

"Just answer the question," Simms said sharply.

"We don't know," Audrey said, shooting a hard look at Simms to prevent him from saying anything more. She got up and went to Elena, crouched at her side. After giving the woman a moment to compose herself, Audrey slipped two pictures of Frost onto the table. One was from Mercury Courier's employee files; the other the photo on the man's license, borrowed from the DMV.

"Ever seen this guy before?"

For a moment Elena just studied the pictures. The way her features were scrunched up, Audrey was certain she was going to shake her head *no* again. They had been through eleven employees already, and none of them had recognized Frost. But then, most of them would never have seen a courier when it was Kendall Sobler who signed for the deliveries.

After a moment Elena Manoff's eyes lit up. "Yes!" she said suddenly. "I remember this guy. It was a while back, so I didn't recognize him at first. He used to be a delivery guy around here, I think. He must have asked Kendall a dozen times to go out with him."

"Did she ever go?" Eckhardt asked quickly.

"A couple of times, I think. Maybe. Like I said, nothing serious. Nice guy, though, if a bit of a noodge. God, what was his name again? Tim? No, was it Mick?"

"It's Vic," Audrey said softly.

"That's it," Elena said, snapping her fingers and nodding with satisfaction. Then her expression changed, her face seemed to lengthen, and her eyes took on a terrible, haunted look.

"Victor Frost?" she asked.

Audrey placed her hand over Elena's and nodded. The other woman looked down at the pictures again, and she began to shake her head and to weep silently. She whispered a word so low her voice could not be heard, but Audrey knew what it was.

Why?

Jenna had too much on her mind to pay close attention to what she was doing in Gross Anatomy lab that Monday afternoon. The lab itself was fine—a fetal pig dissection she could have done, or more accurately, was doing on autopilot—but her thoughts were a cascade of preoccupations. The burned man up in Rockport had lingered with her more than the others, likely because of the handprints on his flesh. One moment she was certain pyrokinesis was the answer, the next she was convinced it was a stupid idea.

Then there was her classwork. She had pretty much caught up with her Spanish assignments, and after class earlier that morning she felt a lot better about how she was doing with her conjugation. She had also had a chance to read *Twelfth Night* over twice more, and was confident she would not embarrass herself too much reading the part of Viola in

Shakespeare class the next day. They were supposed to be sort of acting out *Twelfth Night*—reading aloud from their desks—and she didn't want to stumble over the archaic language.

Then there was Europe from 1815. The test was in two days and though the professor was the best she had ever had, and his lectures engaging enough that they were easy to recall, Jenna did not feel as though she had studied nearly enough.

Work. College. It was hardly as though she needed anything else to think about, but she could not help adding one last thing into the mix: Danny. Their plans over the weekend had been ruined. She had told him she would call to reschedule, but even as they'd had that conversation, she'd wondered again what she thought she was doing. It wasn't a date. There was no doubt in her mind that Danny did not think of it that way. And neither did she.

But maybe there was more to it than just friends. Despite the age difference, and all the reasons she knew she should not even be thinking like that, Jenna could not help wondering what it would be like if she and Danny got together. A completely useless train of thought, but somehow she could not get away from it.

When her lab was over, she headed back to her dorm to call him. Better to just get it over with and stop thinking about it. Even if they were just going to be friends, she supposed that didn't mean she couldn't still daydream about what it would be like if things were different.

No danger in that, right? she asked herself. But even in her mind, she didn't sound convincing.

After she had hit the last number, she slid down to the floor, sitting cross-legged as she listened to the phone ring. On the fourth ring, he answered.

"Detective Mariano."

"Hey. It's Jenna."

"Jenna. Hi. I just got back to the office and was going to call you," Danny said.

"Great minds think alike," she told him, cringing at how silly that sounded.

"Do you know the other half of that expression?" Danny asked. "Michael Feeney, an old Irish friend of mine, always finishes it with: '—and fools seldom differ.' "

"Probably true," Jenna said with a small laugh. "So how do we tell the difference? I mean, how do we know if we're great minds, or fools?"

"That's the mystery of life. You never know," Danny told her.

"Well, that sucks," Jenna replied, and this time they both laughed. "I know you've been working overtime on this case, so dinner's probably out for the moment. Maybe we could sneak in a lunch tomorrow, though?"

"Yeah, that works," Danny replied.

"So how's it going, anyway?" Jenna asked. "With the case, I mean. Anything you can talk about?"

"Ah, it's the same old, same old," Danny said. "State's involved now, so . . . well, let's just say there are a few too many cooks in the kitchen for my taste.

I think it works a lot better when it's just me and Audrey."

"I hear you," Jenna replied.

"So, lunch," Danny went on. "Where did you have in mind?"

"Where would be good for you?" Jenna asked. "I don't want to take you away from work or anything."

As she spoke, she heard a key rattle in the door. The door swung open and Yoshiko entered with a small stack of mail from their box downstairs. With a huff, she slung her backpack off her shoulder and onto the floor. The roomies exchanged silent greetings, but for some reason, Jenna felt just a touch uncomfortable under Yoshiko's gaze.

"We could do Espresso's or Jay's Deli," Danny was saying. "That's convenient for you and I still wouldn't be out of the office more than an hour or so."

Jenna watched as Yoshiko walked to her desk and sat down to sort through the mail.

"Yeah . . . Jay's would be great," Jenna said, eyes on Yoshiko's back. "I've had my share of pizza recently."

Yoshiko turned around and shot Jenna a quizzical glance. Jenna smiled thinly.

"Me, too," Danny said. "Remind me to tell you sometime about this cop up in Rockport. Anyway, is noon too early for you? I'd make it later, but we have to interview some witnesses at one."

"Actually, that works for me," Jenna replied breezily. "But it'll have to be quick. I've got a class at ten to one. So I'll see you then."

They said their good-byes and then Jenna unfolded

herself from her cross-legged position on the floor and hung up the phone before turning to look at Yoshiko.

"What's that look for?" she asked, all innocence.

"What look?" Yoshiko asked, mirroring Jenna's innocent face.

"Can't friends have lunch?" Jenna asked. She knew she sounded defensive, and didn't care.

"Uh-huh," Yoshiko said, nodding slowly but not looking away. "Methinks thou dost protest too much."

Jenna frowned at her. "It's just lunch."

Now the real fun starts! Victor Frost thought gleefully.

He was out back in the kitchen of the Upper Crust Deli and Bakery, dumping the dry ingredients for another batch of pumpernickel into the bread mixer, when he glanced through the order window and saw the two detectives enter. He recognized them immediately, the same two who had interrogated him the other day. He couldn't help but cock a half-smile as he wiped his hands on a dishtowel and walked out from the back room to meet them.

"Victor Frost," the male cop said, sounding all hard and important.

It wasn't a question. They knew exactly who he was, and he knew exactly why they were here. Victor tried to keep the smirk off his face as he nodded quickly, never breaking eye contact with the cop.

And now it's time to play ball!

"We'd like you to come down to the station to answer a few more questions," the male cop said. When he snapped open his ID, Victor caught only a glimpse of his name—Marino . . . Martino . . . Mariano . . . something like that. He didn't remember.

What did it matter?

He was not impressed by the detective's gold shield. It wouldn't have mattered if the guy's name was Sherlock Holmes; he wasn't going to get a thing out of Victor Frost. He had faced down plenty of cops in the past. They tried to be smart, but most of them failed. No, *all* of them failed. No matter how tough they tried to look and act, Victor had known the first time he met these two that they weren't any different.

"I'm in the middle of work here," Victor said with a faux Brooklyn accent as he shrugged and hooked his thumb back at the kitchen. "Can't this wait till I'm off?"

Angelo DeLisle, the owner of the Upper Crust, walked over from the cash register. "Hey, what's the problem?"

The cop flashed a badge for DeLisle. "Detective Mariano. Somerset P.D. We're working in cooperation with the Boston Police, and we need to speak to Mr. Frost," he said.

Angie started to say something, then apparently caught himself and shot a nervous glance at Victor. There was real fear in his eyes, and all Victor could think was, *You miserable little worm! That's your problem right there. You can't let them intimidate you like this.*

Victor was hoping that Angie would show a little spine and stand up to these guys, but instead the man let his shoulders droop and lowered his head. "Just take him and get the hell out of here," he said to the cops under his breath. "This ain't good for business, you comin' in here like this."

As Victor went to get his coat from the locker, the detectives stayed close behind him as if they were afraid he was going to run. They put him into the backseat of a cruiser with a wire cage separating the front seat from the rear. Victor settled into the seat to enjoy the ride to the police station.

It'll be all right, he told himself. *Just like every other time. And if it gets too hot, well, we can always make it even hotter.*

At the station they brought him into the same small, windowless interrogation room he'd been in last time. The only chair was a metal folding job beside a heavy wooden table. On one of the drab, institutional green-painted walls was a reflective mirror.

Victor glanced at his reflection in the mirror and smiled as he ran his fingers through his hair. He knew there was someone—maybe a witness, but certainly another cop or two—behind the glass, watching and analyzing his every move.

He winked.

If these cops really had anything on him, they would have arrested him and read him his rights by now. They were on a fishing expedition, nothing more, and he was going to make sure he played with them plenty without getting hooked.

"Mind if I smoke?" Victor asked, indicating the pack of cigarettes in his shirt pocket.

Victor didn't miss the hint, the flare of curiosity in Mariano's eyes. With a soft chuckle, he lit up, inhaled noisily, then exhaled a billowing plume of blue smoke that he directed at the cop's face.

"We'd like to know where you were last Friday night, between the hours of nine and one in the morning," the female cop—Gaines was her name—said without preamble. Victor had been expecting her to take a softer approach, good cop to Mariano's bad, but her tone was just as harsh as his, if not more so.

After another slow drag, he flicked the lengthening ash of his cigarette onto the scuffed tile floor. He rocked back in the chair and frowned as though deep in thought, then sadly shook his head.

"Can't say I remember," he said, and scratched his nose with his thumb. The smoke from his cigarette curled up around his face, making him squint. "Probably home in bed asleep. Why?"

"Any chance you were up in Rockport?"

Victor narrowed his eyes, then shook his head again slowly. "Summer place, ain't it? Why would I want to go there in the winter?"

"To visit an old friend of yours," Mariano said. He leaned forward, poised like a tiger ready to pounce. "A man named Matthew Dahms."

"Old Man Dahmsie?" Victor said, feigning surprise. "He still living up there? I would've thought he'd move to Florida or Arizona, now that he's retired."

"He's not retired anymore," Gaines said, all seriousness. "He's dead. He was burned to death on Friday night. But then you know that, don't you? You'd kind of have to, seeing as how you killed him."

Victor inhaled, and held the smoke in his lungs. It had only been a matter of time, he knew, before they would connect what he'd done in Rockport to what he'd done in Somerset and Boston. And here it was. Still, though, they were just fishing. All they had was circumstantial evidence.

"You think just 'cause I knew the guy, I'm the one who killed him?" Victor asked, scoffing at them. Thick smoke spilled from his mouth as he spoke. "Knew a postman down in Sarasota drove his car into a tree. I was about eight. You think I killed him, too? Look, I'm not even sure where Old Man Dahms lives—uh, lived," he said. "And maybe you should tell me why I would want to kill him in the first place."

He had to work hard to keep from laughing out loud.

"We'll get to that in a bit," Gaines said mildly, but she and her partner exchanged a glance that told Victor he had them.

"We know that you worked for Mr. Dahms," Mariano said evenly. "Just like we know you once dated Kendall Sobler. She dumped you, and maybe you didn't like it when she found a new guy."

"I dated Kendall, sure," Victor said easily. "But I broke up with her, not the other way around."

Mariano smiled. "You don't really think we buy that, do you? Sobler only went out with you out of pity in the first place. We've got signed affidavits to that effect."

Victor laughed and shook his head. "You two are something else," he muttered, unable to believe the cop was smug enough to think crap like that would get under his skin.

"We have you connected to all three of these murder victims, and in all three cases, you haven't been able to offer a convincing alibi," Gaines told him.

Victor took a drag on his cigarette, then blew some truly pitiful smoke rings. He had never been good at that. He ignored both detectives.

Mariano slapped his palm loudly on the table. He leaned close to Victor, glaring at him almost nose to nose . . . so close Victor thought he could just about smell the doughnuts.

"It's just a matter of time," Mariano said. "We're going to nail you, Frost. Trust me on this one."

Victor thought again about the doughnuts and forced himself not to laugh. The intensity in the room was so high he knew they would take it as all but an admission of guilt if he so much as blinked his eyes wrong. As the cop slowly backed down, Victor took another slow drag from his cigarette and then, reaching forward, crushed it out in the ashtray on the table.

"If you're so sure I killed these people," he said softly, letting the smoke drift lazily out of his mouth and nose, "arrest me."

He held his hands out, wrists together as though ready to be handcuffed.

"I *dare* you." He was pleased to see that Mariano was trembling because he wanted so much to hit him, not just arrest him, but neither he nor his partner reached for their cuffs.

"I think I'll go now, then." He pushed the chair back so hard it fell back and clattered on the floor. As he stood up, he kept staring straight at Mariano.

He was privately thrilled that he had brought the detective to this point. It had almost been too easy. But Victor was a little disappointed, as well, that he hadn't been able to goad Mariano into actually slugging him. *That* would have been the frosting on the cake, to make this guy snap, but Mariano stepped back.

"Yeah, you can leave," Mariano said, his voice low and controlled. "But you'll be back."

Victor met Mariano's hate-filled gaze with a grin. He let his smile widen until he knew it was the biggest, goofiest expression he could manage. He wanted to say something, just to rub it in a little more, but stopped himself.

Whistling a happy tune, he slung his coat over his shoulder, opened the door, and walked out of the interrogation room. He shook another cigarette into his hand, slid the pack back into his shirt pocket, then stuck the butt between his lips. Even before he tucked the pack back into his pocket, the tip of the cigarette lit up, and smoke slipped back over his shoulder like a trailing scarf.

The instant she opened the first of the several plastic evidence bags they had gotten from the Somerset P.D., the smell of burned fabric blew into Jenna's face so strongly it made her stomach turn. The nausea steadily increased as she carefully spread out the remains of Kendall Sobler's burned winter jacket on the examination table. The outer layer of the coat was black and as thin as charred paper with crispy, jagged edges. It crumbled to powder at even the gentlest touch.

"This isn't going to be easy," Jenna said, taking short, shallow breaths as she and Slick leaned forward and stared intently at the scorched fabric.

"No, but try to picture in your mind what happened," Slick said, keeping his attention focused on the material. "If you were to pass by someone in a crowd and didn't want to draw too much attention to yourself, where would you touch them or brush up against them?"

"Probably the arm or shoulder," Jenna said. "Or maybe the back. Or the . . . maybe you should check her pants."

"Uh-huh," Slick murmured, nodding slightly.

With the delicate touch Jenna had seen so often when he was performing an autopsy, Slick removed the dead woman's pants from the evidence bag they were sealed in. He carefully turned them over so they were facedown. After adjusting the light, he leaned forward and examined the burned fabric, tracing over it—but not touching it—with the tip of his forefinger.

Jenna was trying her best to see anything that might be a pattern in the burns, but all she could see was the charred, flaking mess of ash. It was hard to believe that this had ever been an article of clothing.

Using a pair of forceps, Slick lifted up first one leg, then the other. The material made loud crinkling sounds that for a sickening instant reminded Jenna of the sound breakfast cereal made when she first poured milk onto it. Again, the sour tightening gripped her stomach, and a bad taste rose up into the back of her throat.

"Hmmm . . . yes. Have a look at this," Slick said.

He carefully laid the pants down, left hip exposed. With his forceps, he pointed to a place on the fabric. At first, Jenna couldn't see what he was indicating, but then—suddenly—it snapped into focus. On the seat of the blackened material, there was a small, scorched swatch with a bubbled ring surrounding the perimeter. The M.E. took a magnifying glass and examined it more closely, then let Jenna do the same. She saw where the material had burned away, leaving the tracing of the fabric's weave like a fine gray mesh of ashes.

"It definitely looks as though that small section was heated more than the rest of the pants," she said.

She didn't want to jump to any conclusions, so she refrained from saying anything more as she began to open another evidence bag. This one was marked SPORTS COAT. Below that, written in bold, black ink, was the name ALAN NASH along with the case number, date, time, and location that the evidence had been collected. Jenna carefully removed the article of clothing from the bag and placed it on the table.

Without a word, Slick set to examining it. He carefully turned the burned material over and, using the magnifying glass again, examined the cloth for several minutes. Finally he looked up at Jenna and said, "Take a look here."

Jenna's hand trembled slightly as she took the magnifying glass from him and looked where Slick was pointing. It didn't take long this time to see it. Just like on Kendall's pants, there was a small circular area that definitely looked like it had burned hotter than the rest of the material. Where the fabric looked almost as if it had *melted,* instead of just burned.

"If we're right about all this, that definitely would be where the flames began," Jenna said softly. The evidence was right there in front of them. As badly burned as both articles of clothing were, they each had a melted scorch mark that indicated some type of superheating in one area.

But is it really possible that someone could do something like that, make a person ignite with just a touch? Jenna wondered. A bone-deep chill rippled up her back.

It was too weird, too difficult to imagine; but something else about this bothered her. Bad enough to believe that someone would be capable of setting a person on fire just by touching him, but something else didn't seem right.

"Wait a second," she whispered. She leaned forward and spread the remains of Alan Nash's jacket out on the table, then stood back and, hand on her chin, studied them for a moment.

"What is it, Jenna?" Slick asked.

She could hear the tone of expectation in his voice, but she focused all her attention on the burned clothing.

What else isn't right about this?

"It's not just where they caught fire," she finally said, hearing the distant, almost dreamy tone in her voice as she tried to find a way to express the *wrongness* of what she saw. "It's not just that . . . it's also the rest of the clothing."

"How do you mean?" Slick frowned as he looked up at her.

Biting down on her lower lip, Jenna gazed at him, afraid for just an instant that he might laugh at her suggestion. But she knew better. Dr. Slikowski trusted and admired her for her intuition and insight, had more faith in her than she did in herself.

"We know that these clothes weren't treated with any chemicals, right?" she asked.

Narrowing his eyes, still obviously not sure where she was taking this, Slick nodded slowly. "They tested for everything that seemed likely and found nothing."

"But other than those tiny, individual superheated spots, where we think the victims were touched," Jenna said, "the clothing is burned evenly . . . *absolutely* evenly, just like the bodies were." She took a breath before continuing. "It looks to me like the fire didn't spread out over the victims. It's almost as if, once he touched them, the flames just 'appeared,' all at once, consuming everything in an instant."

Slick looked up at her, dumbfounded, and for once had absolutely nothing to say.

chapter 10

The weekend snowstorm had left its mark on the city, and though the streets weren't quite as messy as they had been the day before, only a superficial job had been done of clearing them.

They're getting lazy, banking that a warm day or two'll come along and melt it off, Danny thought as he stared at the snowbank built up along the sidewalk.

Beyond it, the brownstone building he and Audrey were staking out was mostly dark. It was after two in the morning, and most everyone would be asleep by now. On the third floor, where Victor Frost had his apartment, the blue light of a television flickered in one of the windows.

Thoughts of Frost made him heave an angry sigh.

"That wasn't your stomach growling," Audrey said.

Danny glanced at her, allowed himself a small smile. "No, it wasn't my stomach."

"I thought we agreed you weren't going to sweat Frost's little comedy show today?" Audrey asked, studying him closely. Her frown deepened. "Look, Danny, the guy had our number, all right? We know he's it, now more than ever. We've dealt with stone-cold bad guys before, haven't we? So Captain Wessell thinks we could have gone at him harder. Let him give Frost a State Police interrogation then. Gonci and Boggs were both watching, and they're both on our side."

"We should've had Boggs in there with us," Danny said absently, tapping his fingers on the steering wheel. "Not that I want to give the interview over to Boston P.D., but Lieutenant Boggs is a pretty scary-looking individual. Maybe he could've—"

"Danny," Audrey snapped.

He gripped the steering wheel and turned to her. Audrey was staring at him, obviously exasperated.

"Drop it," she told him firmly. "We ran a solid interview. We've got no concrete evidence on the guy and we tried to see if we could get him skittish, get him talking. We didn't. He's smarter than that. Fine. Now we've got to do it the hard way. If he's not at work, we have to know where he is. That means stake-out. Long, boring hours together. I don't want to spend them talking about how much you wanted to throttle the guy 'cause he was teasing us in the inter-view. I need you grounded, back to earth, on the job."

Eyes closed, teeth clenched, Danny sighed and then blew out a frustrated breath. When he opened his eyes, Audrey was watching him expectantly.

"Okay," he said, and nodded. "Okay, I'm with you. I just hate it that he's waving it in our faces like this."

"He's a showoff," Audrey replied, and shrugged. "Let him show it off, then. Frost is so cocky he's bound to lose it. We just have to make sure he does it before anyone else ends up dead."

"Yeah, easy for you to say." Danny leaned his chin on the steering wheel and looked out the windshield again at the brownstone just a little way up the street. The blue light was gone. "TV's off. He must have finally gone to sleep."

"Lucky him," Audrey said.

"What time are Simms and Eckhardt supposed to take over?"

"Not until five."

"Beautiful. I've got lunch with Jenna at noon. I'm sure I'll be at my best." Danny yawned, as if to punctuate his complaint. Though he was watching Frost's apartment building, out of the corner of his eye he noticed that Audrey was staring at him.

With a quizzical expression, he turned to face her. "What? I'll stop harping on Frost, okay? Quit looking at me like that."

"I'm past the Frost thing," Audrey told him. "What's this about Jenna?"

Danny frowned. He glanced quickly out the window at their suspect's residence, then back at Audrey. "We're having lunch today. What's the problem with that?"

"You two have been getting pretty cozy lately." Audrey watched him, studied his face. "Or I guess I should say, you're getting cozy *again*."

Danny stared at her. "Hold on a second—"

"Just because she's now nineteen," Audrey interrupted, "I don't see how that makes a whole lot of difference. Nothing has changed."

He turned to stare out at the street, at the mounds of snow and the darkened windows of the building where their suspect, a multiple murderer capable of setting people on fire with the power of his mind—or so they thought—was probably even now sleeping quite restfully. Frost was warm and dreaming inside. Danny could see his own breath in the car, and he wasn't allowed to go to sleep because of Frost.

Perspective, he told himself. *Keep it in perspective.*

"Audrey, listen," he said and sighed. "I know that you wouldn't approve if something were to happen between Jenna and me."

"I think Jenna's amazing," Audrey said quickly. "Let's be clear on that. I like her, and I envy her mind. But—"

"But she's nineteen," Danny finished for her. "Yes, I know. Did you think I'd forgotten? You don't approve. The job wouldn't approve. You're looking out for me, and maybe for Jenna, too, but if you want to do something to help, if you're really looking out for me—"

Audrey leaned forward ever so slightly, brows furrowed in an expression of concern.

"Then back off," Danny finished, allowing anger into his tone.

"Whoa, partner," Audrey said, holding up a hand. "Maybe you'd better think—"

"I am thinking," Danny snapped at her.

Audrey flinched, surprised at his vehemence, but he pressed on.

"I told you about what happened with me and Kim. It isn't like that with Jenna. She *gets* it. You haven't had a boyfriend for more than two months in the last four years, so I *know* you know what I'm talking about. If Jenna were six years older, I'd have jumped at the chance to have a relationship with her. But that's a big 'if.' I'm not going to do anything stupid."

Danny contemplated a moment, stared out at Frost's brownstone. He turned the key backward in the ignition so that he could roll the window down a little. Fresh air might help clear his head.

"You want to know what really bothers me? That I know she cares about me, and I could follow up on that, make something of it, and because of the age difference, she could really regret it later. I couldn't deal with that. So I'll be her friend, and I'll enjoy her company, and I'll be nice to her when she has a new boyfriend. And that's that."

"Is it?" Audrey asked.

"It'll have to be."

At a quarter to six in the morning, the dawn still just a tease but hinting at sunshine, Danny parked his

Cutlass in the small lot behind 76 Lawson Road, the building where he had had an apartment for going on five years. It was on the Cambridge side of Somerset, not far from Lafford Square, on a side street that was residential enough to have trees and small yards in front of the buildings.

As he walked around to the front, Danny's mind strayed back to the conversation he and Audrey had had about Jenna. He figured it revealed a lot about how much she meant to him. Jenna was the one topic that could have derailed his ranting about Victor Frost. In some ways, he regretted having opened up to Audrey about his feelings. She was his partner, yes, and his best friend as well. But he figured everybody had thoughts and emotions that were best held back, like in a hand of poker. Plus he knew that Audrey would judge, might even treat Jenna differently the more time he spent with her.

"She's just a kid, she's just a kid, she's just a kid," Danny muttered aloud as he stepped onto the badly shoveled path from the driveway. The tiny front yard had nearly a foot of snow on it, and piled higher around the path. Parts of it had been trammeled by people and dogs, and he was pretty sure he saw a patch of yellow snow ten feet away.

Winter, he thought. *Great for a couple of months, then it's like hell, without the floor show.*

Danny yawned again, bleary-eyed and muddled from exhaustion, and he had a lunch date with Jenna in six hours. Four hours sleep would have to do.

There had been plenty of times when he had been forced to get by on even less.

Sleep, lunch with Jenna, and then back on the case, first digging into Frost's life, then staking out the pyro's apartment after he got off work at the bakery. *Pyro.* That's what he was, really. Pyromaniac. He got off on the fires, Danny was sure of that, and on the killings as well.

Off to his left, across the street from his building, a car door slammed. The sky had lightened enough so that when Danny glanced over that way and saw the man walking toward him from the dark red Nissan, he knew exactly who it was.

Victor Frost.

The killer strutted toward him, already draped with the apron he would have to wear for work at the bakery that day.

Time to make the doughnuts, Danny thought wildly. His right hand slipped behind him; his fingers caressed the service weapon clipped onto his belt in its small holster. Frost walked up the driveway, smiling at him, eyes bright though the day was still just beginning. He turned down the path and Danny faced him.

"That's far enough," Danny instructed him.

Frost paused, a wounded expression on his face. "I'm hurt, Detective Mariano. After all you put me through yesterday, and all those hours you spent sitting outside my apartment last night and this morning, and you can't even give me five minutes of your time. I think I may have an idea who killed those people."

The pyro grinned.

"I know who killed those people," Danny snapped. "And you better state your business and go on your way, Mr. Frost."

"Or what?" Frost asked. "You'll shoot me or arrest me? On what charges? Okay, harassment, maybe, but it'd never stick. Besides, I'm only here to help."

Danny frowned, flexed his hand but kept it right where it was behind his back, hovering over his gun. "All right, then. Talk. Tell me who killed Alan Nash. Who killed Kendall Sobler and Matthew Dahms?"

"I can tell you who killed them and why they're being killed. If you want to know badly enough."

"You like games, don't you, Frost?" Danny prodded. "Tell you what. I'm tired and in no mood for games. You come on down to my office when you get out of work today, then you can tell me whatever this big insight of yours is."

Frost laughed. "Now who's playing the game, Detective? God, give me a break. You're dying to hear what I've got to say, and don't try to deny it. By the way, you'd be surprised, I think, how easy it was to track you down," Frost told him, his voice dropping a bit, both deeper and quieter.

Danny's fingers tightened on the grip of his gun, and he snapped the strap off with his thumb.

"Enough games. Say what you came to say, or I'm going inside. I need my beauty rest."

That seemed to strike Frost as amusing, for he laughed again. Danny shivered at the sound, so eerie was the man's amusement.

"I'll tell you what," Frost promised. "Just come a little closer, I'll whisper it in your ear."

Danny blinked. For the first time since Frost had approached, his fear surfaced.

"You want me closer?" he asked. Then he pulled his pistol and held it against his hip as he took three steps. "I'm closer."

"Oooh, a gun," Frost cooed. "How quaint. I've never actually seen one up close. Could I?"

"In about thirty seconds, you're going to whether you want to or not," Danny vowed.

"You should have shot me." Frost thrust out a hand and grabbed the front of his jacket. Danny tried to bring his gun up, reacting as quickly as he could. The grin on Frost's face taunted him.

Then Danny Mariano's entire body burst into flames; his clothes were blazing up around him, his hair was on fire, and he felt the flesh of his face begin to sear with the heat. The fire was consuming him . . . and as he flailed at it, tossing his gun down, he saw Victor Frost hurrying back down the driveway, hands in his pockets, whistling like he had not a care in the world.

Between them, the snow.

With a roar of fury and agony, Danny hurled himself into the deep snow on the front yard and began to roll in it. The fire melted snow all around him, hissing as it became steam.

The flames went out. A car engine choked to life and then chugged away.

Numb with pain, his mind in a fog, Danny felt his eyes start to close, and his vision began to fade.

Fade to black.

Audrey's eyes snapped open. *Something. What was it?*

The knock came again, dulled by the distance between her front door and her bedroom. Whoever it was, he was persistent. Only a few seconds went by before the knocking resumed. Even religious zealots preaching door to door weren't that pushy.

With a groan, she sat up in bed and rubbed at her eyes. Dragging her whole body like dead weight, she rose and pulled on a robe as she zombie-walked, barefoot, out of her bedroom and down the hall, past the kitchen and living room and to the interior door. Audrey lived in the upstairs half of a duplex. She had her own entrance, but there were all those stairs, and she had never gotten around to installing an intercom. It seemed kind of lazy not to just go down and answer it.

Unless it's eight A.M. and you've had less than an hour's sleep, she thought.

She opened the door at the top of the stairs and started down. Her visitor knocked again, and Audrey called down that she was coming, to hold it down.

At the bottom, she cinched her robe tight and looked through the peephole.

Lieutenant Gonci stood on her Welcome mat, a

grim expression on his face. Audrey worked the triple lock in seconds and hauled the door open. Gonci had his fist raised to knock again and seemed almost startled that she had finally opened the door.

"Oh," he grunted. "Detective Gaines . . . Audrey, I . . ."

Something terrible has happened to Danny, she thought. Her stomach churned, and she thought she was going to throw up. Audrey had never been so afraid before in her life, not even the time she had a killer's gleaming blade thrust into her.

"Just tell me," she said quickly, "is he alive?"

Gonci seemed to deflate, all the pressure of having to carry a tragic message suddenly released. He nodded. "Danny's alive. He's in ICU with some bad burns. They don't know yet how extensive the damage is."

Audrey only heard one word.

Burns.

Without another word to her lieutenant, she turned to go back up the stairs, taking them two at a time. Gonci followed. She knew he was speaking, but she wasn't listening. Audrey hurried to her bedroom, threw off her robe and pulled on blue jeans and a gray Somerset P.D. sweatshirt. She put on clean socks and sneakers, then clipped a holster to the back of her belt and slipped her service weapon into it. With a quick glance around the room, she located her shoulder holster and slipped that on as well, filling it with her backup weapon, a .38 she usually only fired at the range.

In silence, she stormed out of her room and was almost startled to find Gonci standing in the middle of her apartment, waiting for her to appear.

"Where do you think you're going?" he demanded.

Audrey frowned, but said nothing. It was almost as though he were speaking some other language, and she could not communicate with him.

"Listen to me, Audrey," the lieutenant said, positioning himself between her and the door. "Hold on a second."

"No, *you* hold on," she snapped, hearing her voice crack with emotion and hating it. "My partner just got torched by a skel who has committed multiple murders here, and in California, and probably more we don't know about. He's gotten away with it before, but not this time." She pushed her emotions down deep; at least the soft ones. The hard ones she would be needing shortly.

As Audrey pushed past the lieutenant, he grabbed her shoulder in a surprisingly strong grip and spun her around. He held her with both hands.

"Go to the hospital," he said sternly. "You're no good to him like this. We don't have any witnesses putting Frost at the scene, and no other evidence so far."

"I don't need evidence to know he did it," Audrey sneered. "Now get your goddamn hands off me. This is my partner we're talking about here."

"I know that. For God's sake, I know that," Gonci said, his voice still steady. He took his hands away and just looked at her. "But Audrey, if you pick him up now, haul him in again, it's going to hurt the case against him, not help. Especially if you give him a little tune-up in the process. You know as well as I do, if you want to help Danny, you've got to do it by the book. You go to the hospital, and let me handle it. We'll get the bastard, I promise."

Audrey stared at him, fury still emanating from her in waves. Then, suddenly, it all left her in a rush and she felt weaker than she ever had before, almost as though she might faint.

"But he's my partner," she said, voice barely above a whisper.

Gonci put one hand on the back of her neck and pulled her forward so she could lay her head on his shoulder.

"I know," the lieutenant whispered. "We'll get him, Audrey. I swear we will. You go to the hospital, make sure the guy doesn't take a second crack at him. Right now, Danny may be our best chance of making this case. If he can identify Frost, then it's all over."

"Oh, God, Danny." Audrey shuddered, then stood up straighter and nodded. "I'm gonna go take care of my partner."

Jenna sat in a booth at Jay's Deli, long past annoyed. She knew that something must have happened with the case, or Danny would have been there. But she also knew that he could have called, and the guys behind the counter would have given her a message, let her know he wasn't coming.

And he wasn't coming, that much was clear.

They were supposed to have met at noon. It was five past one. Jenna had already missed the beginning of her Medical Anthropology class. If she hurried, she might be able to catch the second half, but what was the point? The last thing she wanted was the professor to see her walking in thirty or forty minutes late. Besides, Roseanne would take notes. They were supposed to walk in the morning, and Jenna could ask her then.

But he's not coming, she thought again, for perhaps the thousandth time. *I can't believe he didn't even call.*

She had ordered some fries and a soda to tide her over, and now it looked as though that was her lunch. As she got up to pay at the counter, leaving a couple of dollars' tip on the table, Jenna felt a twinge of dread in her heart.

She couldn't believe he would not have found a way to get a message to her. He was a Somerset cop, after all. It wasn't as though he could not have gotten cooperation from any of the merchants in the area to get a message to her, even if the phone at Jay's was broken.

In despair, she walked back up Carpenter Street and then cut across campus to Sparrow Hall. She would have to go to work soon, but not without checking her messages. At the very least, Danny would have left her a message on her machine.

But there was no message.

Something's wrong, she thought, feeling a cold twist in her stomach.

She picked up the phone and dialed Danny's num-

ber at the police station. There was no answer. She
hung up before the beep. What would she say in a
message, just give him a hard time for not showing
up? No. He'd call. She had to go to work now, but
Danny knew where to find her.

He'll call.

chapter 11

It was a beautiful afternoon. The air was warm, and the sun, lowering in the west, reflected brightly off the snow. Jenna knew that she should be feeling great, but as she walked down the hill to work, she couldn't get rid of the nagging feeling that something was wrong.

Something *had* to be wrong.

Danny wouldn't have blown off their lunch date like this without calling her or getting a message to her somehow. By the time she had keyed the door lock and entered Slick's office, she was feeling almost sick with worry.

As she stepped into the main office, Jenna noticed that there was no music coming from the office sound system, so she assumed that Slick was out of the office at a lecture or consultation, possibly downstairs doing an autopsy. Just the same, she glanced into his office and was startled when she saw him sitting silently in his wheelchair behind his desk. He had his elbows resting on the arms of the chair, his chin propped on his folded hands as he stared straight ahead.

"Oh . . . I didn't think you were here," Jenna said, her voice catching slightly from her surprise.

For a terrible moment Slick didn't say a word, not even a greeting as he sat there regarding her. He narrowed his eyes and nodded his head slightly. His face was drawn and pale, and heavy shadows hung under the eyes.

"Wha . . . what's the matter?" Jenna asked. The sourness in her stomach rose, making a bad taste in the back of her throat.

"You might want to sit down, Jenna," Slick said. His voice was quiet and restrained. "I have some bad news."

A tingling wave of panic raced through her, but she remained standing by the door. She took a deep breath, bracing herself for the worst.

"Is it Danny?" she asked, trembling inside. "Did something happen to Danny?" Her throat felt dry and tight, as if someone had a stranglehold on it.

Slick blinked in surprise, then his expression softened and the corners of his mouth drooped sadly.

"How did you know?"

Jenna suddenly found that she could not catch her breath. Moving slowly, almost mechanically, she pulled the guest chair away from the wall and slowly sank down into it. Her chest and stomach filled with a terrible, cold emptiness. She felt cold and numb and hollow, as if the world had somehow collapsed and was closing in on her. She tried to clear her mind and focus her thoughts, desperate to form words so she could ask Dr. Slikowski exactly what had happened, but she was swept away by the terrible conviction that Danny was dead.

Tears blurred her vision as they ran in hot streams down her face, but she felt curiously detached from them, distant, as though they were someone else's tears. Only half a year ago, her best friend, Melody, had been murdered, and it had torn her up inside. If Danny were dead now, too, then all the tears she could ever cry wouldn't be enough.

"Early this morning," Slick continued, his voice low but strong, her comfort, "a neighbor found him in the front yard of his apartment building. He was unconscious."

"Oh, God . . . *no!*" Jenna whispered, barely registering the words as she covered her mouth with both hands and stared blankly ahead at Slick. She felt like she would throw up.

"He was burned," Slick said. "He's here, in the burn unit, but he's in . . . his condition is very serious."

"Then he . . . he's alive?" Jenna asked, finding that slim ray of hope almost impossible to grasp on to and hold.

"Yes. He's still alive," Slick echoed softly. His eyes were filled with sadness as he rolled his wheelchair around the desk and moved toward her. Jenna felt too numb to move as he reached out and wrapped his arms around her. She pressed her face hard against his shoulder, feeling the rough texture of his sports coat.

"Oh, God, why?" she murmured. "Why do I have to lose everyone I ever get close to?"

"It's not your fault, Jenna," Slick said, and she couldn't miss the slight edge in his voice. "It's part of his job. He puts his life on the line every day he goes to work. You know that, and he knows that. He knows the risks."

"I know, I know," Jenna said, though she shook her head as if to deny it. "But it's just not . . ." She let the words trail off. *Fair?* she thought. *Was I going to say fair?* She was almost angry with herself for being so naïve. The world was not fair.

"How did it happen?" she asked, feeling a kind of chill calm begin to sweep through her.

"The police are investigating it with every resource they have, and the doctors are doing everything they can. We have one of the best burn units in the country," Slick replied. His voice sounded faint, even though his mouth was inches from her ear. "He was lucky in at least one regard."

It took a moment for his words to register, but finally Jenna broke off their embrace and sat back to stare blankly at her boss. Her vision was blurred with tears, making shattered rays of light dance around his head almost as though he had a halo.

"What do you mean . . . lucky?" she rasped.

"He's lucky that it snowed the other day, and that there was still plenty of it on the ground," Slick explained softly. "Whatever happened to him, and I have no doubt that the police will find out, he had the presence of mind to drop and roll in the snow to extinguish the flames."

Though she still felt completely numb, Jenna nodded as she tried to let his words sink in.

"I have to go," she said. "I have to see him."

"I'll go with you," Slick said. "The burn unit is on the fourth floor. But I have to warn you, Jenna. It's too early to tell how things will turn out. A significant portion of his body was burned, and he still hasn't regained consciousness."

Wide-eyed, Jenna only nodded and wiped again at her tears.

This can't be happening!

But it was. Grief gripped her with icy hands.

"Take all the time you need to compose yourself." Slick reached back to take a handful of tissues from the box on his desk and handed them to her.

"I . . . I don't know if I can take this," she whispered hoarsely.

The muscles in Audrey's neck and shoulders were tensed so tightly they hurt. She knew she had to loosen up—that anybody wound this tight was bound to snap—but she could not help it. Her knuckles ached as she gripped the steering wheel of her car and leaned forward to stare up at the third-floor windows of the dilapidated brownstone.

Accept it. He's not home, she told herself.

But if Victor Frost wasn't home, he hadn't been at

work, either. She had swung by the Upper Crust Bakery first thing that afternoon after stopping by the hospital to check to see how Danny was doing.

No change there.

He was still unconscious, and the doctors were preparing him for an operation later that afternoon. There was nothing Audrey could do for him at the hospital, so she figured to hell with what Lieutenant Gonci had said. The one thing she *could* do was go looking for Victor Frost.

But if he isn't home and he isn't at work, then where is he?

He had to be somewhere. Audrey tried to ignore the nagging fear that he had taken off. Maybe he'd done what he'd intended to do, killed everyone he'd planned to kill, and was now content to disappear.

But Audrey doubted it.

Something—and she wanted to believe that it was more than wishful thinking—was telling her that Frost wasn't finished yet. He'd stick around, at least for a while, if only to gloat over the damage he'd done. A freak like Victor Frost wasn't just happy with hurting people. He had to revel in the pain for a while.

All Audrey had to do was find him before he torched anyone else, but she wasn't sure what she would do if she did. Her first impulse was to kill him, just shoot him with a throwaway piece she'd picked up off a skel in a narcotics bust in '97 and had in a shoebox in her linen closet at home. There was a landfill in Chelsea she figured already had a body or two decaying in it. One more couldn't hurt. A monster like Frost, it was what he deserved, especially after what he'd done to Danny. She had seen a lot of misery and suffering in her years on the job, but the attack on Danny had her nerves frayed like nothing else had.

You can't kill him, she told herself. *You'd have to live with yourself afterward.*

And that would not be easy.

No, when it came down to it, Audrey doubted that she could bring herself to kill Frost, no matter how much he deserved it. But just the same, she hoped that she or some other member of the task force would be put into a position where they didn't have a choice, that Frost would force it and end up with a bullet in the head.

Audrey waited a few minutes more as she stared up at the empty third-floor windows. Finally she took a deep calming breath, held it for a moment, then let it out slowly as she turned the key and started up the car. She was about to shift and pull away from the curb when she saw a familiar figure coming up the sidewalk toward her. He had a small bag of groceries clutched tightly to his chest and was walking with a peculiar jolly bounce in his step.

Come on, you bastard. Give me one good reason, Audrey thought as she turned off the ignition, opened the car door, and stepped out onto the street. The cold air made her catch her breath as she straightened up and loosened her service revolver in its holster.

Frost hadn't noticed her yet, but she never took her eyes off him as she swung the car door shut. His eyes were narrowed from the glare of the sun, and he was whistling an off-key tune as he walked down the sidewalk as if he didn't have a care in the world.

"Police officer," Audrey shouted as she stepped around the car and into his path, hand on her weapon. "Do. Not. Move."

For a single instant, their eyes met, freezing them both in time. Then, without a word, Frost dropped his bag of groceries, turned, and started to run.

Go on, rabbit, she thought. *You just bought a bullet.*

"Hold it! Stop or I'll shoot!" Audrey shouted as she drew her gun and aimed at his back.

Frost was moving fast, but something in her tone of voice must have told him that she meant business because he drew to a stop, his feet skidding on the asphalt. Without turning around, he raised both hands above his head.

Damn you, Audrey thought.

Weapon gripped with both hands, Audrey cautiously approached him. A few passersby had noticed the activity and had stopped to watch, but they were all keeping a respectful distance. Or more likely a fearful one.

"Turn around slowly, and keep your hands in the air," Audrey commanded.

She drew a bead on his back and could feel a twitch in her trigger finger as he slowly turned. When he faced her again, he had a wide, goofy grin.

"Why, Detective Gaines," Frost said, his voice

loaded with sarcasm as he squinted at her in the sunlight. "How nice to see you again."

"Not a word, Frost," Audrey said as she approached him.

And realized she had no idea what to do next.

She should have called for backup before she left the car. If Audrey needed another object lesson about not reacting out of emotion, this was it. All along she had considered the theory that Frost might be pyrokinetic to be absolutely ridiculous. Now, though, face to face with the guy, she hesitated.

What if it's true?

No other explanation really fit the evidence. Danny was another example. If Frost really could set her on fire just by touching her and thinking about it, she could not afford to get too close to him. How, then, to bring him in?

Should have pulled the trigger when you had the chance, she told herself.

But she had hesitated. Even if he had fled and disobeyed an officer of the law, even if he was a suspect in several murders, shooting an apparently unarmed man in the back was just not an option.

Now, faced off against him, even though the law was on her side, she was powerless.

"Any particular reason why your first response is to run away from the police?" she asked.

"You're not exactly my favorite person to bump into," Frost said. There was a malicious gleam in his eye that Audrey couldn't miss. "And my guess is that this is not a social call."

"That's up to you," Audrey said through clenched teeth. "For starters, why don't you tell me where you were around five o'clock this morning."

"Is this an official interrogation, Detective?" Frost said archly. "Am I under arrest? Because if I am, then I believe you have to read me my rights, and I'm supposed to have my lawyer present."

Audrey's hands were beginning to ache from holding the gun so tightly, but she didn't dare lower it, much less put it away. "I *know* you did it."

"Did what?" Frost said, looking at her with a twisted, irritating smirk on his face. "I have no idea what you're talking about, Detective Gaines, but if you don't mind, I'd like to be on my way."

"On your way to jail, maybe," Audrey snapped, "unless California extradites you first. Then it could be death row."

"Are you threatening me, Detective Gaines? In front of all these witnesses?"

Frost indicated the onlookers with a wide sweep of his hand. His smug look of triumph was enough to send Audrey's blood pressure rocketing. No matter how hard she tried, she couldn't stop her hands from trembling.

He tried to kill Danny! she thought, and as much as she hated herself for it, she wanted desperately— right now—to pull the trigger and erase the stain of Victor Frost from the earth.

"Detective, you're not even in your own jurisdiction here, so why don't you get off my back and go home to Somerset . . . unless you want to face some charges of your own. We could start with harassment and police brutality." Frost was smiling widely as he slowly extended his right hand and took a few steps closer to her, but he stopped short when Audrey jabbed her revolver at him.

"Not another step, mister," she said, her voice hard with command. "I want some answers. Where were you early this morning?"

Frost glared at her, then shrugged. "I don't have to answer that," he said casually. "And I have things to do, so I think I'll be on my way."

Audrey took a few quick steps backward as he moved past her and bent down to pick up the bag of groceries he'd dropped. Something wet was leaking out of the bottom of the bag, leaving a dark stain on the sidewalk.

"Ohh, now look at that, will you," he said, his voice tinged with mock sorrow. "My eggs got broken when I dropped them." He reached into the bag, scooped up a handful of broken shells and yolk, and flicked them onto the pavement. "I should charge your department to replace them."

In the coldest voice she could summon up from within her, Audrey bluffed. "Detective Mariano is awake, Frost. And he's already identified you as his assailant."

Frost flinched. It wasn't much, but she couldn't miss it. She was pleased to see that she had gotten to him. In an instant, his whole demeanor changed as he stood up slowly and glared at her.

"You don't want to push me, Detective Gaines," he

said, trembling with repressed rage as he pointed a finger at her and shook it. "I mean it. You *don't* want to push me."

Audrey's body was rigid with tension, and she didn't back down even an inch. She kept staring at him with a cold, cruel look that she knew was getting to him.

"He didn't die from the burns," she said softly, pushing the raw nerve she'd found. "Too bad for you."

For a moment or two, Frost's expression was unreadable, but then the corners of his mouth twitched into a twisted half-smile.

"You'd be arresting me if he was awake. No," he said evenly, his eyes flat and glassy. "Not possible," he said. "I guess it's too bad for *you.*"

And with that, he turned around and walked away from her. Audrey was powerless to do anything but watch him go. Once he had walked up the stairway and entered his apartment building, she got back into her car and radioed the Boston P.D. She was trembling terribly as she requested that the police put around-the-clock surveillance on Victor Frost to make sure he didn't skip town. Now that she had turned up the heat, she wasn't about to let things cool down.

Her stomach filled with a sour churning as she started up the car and pulled slowly away from the curb. As she drove through city traffic down to Storrow Drive, she fought to hold back the emotions that welled up inside her, but she knew she couldn't keep them buried for long. Crossing the Longfellow Bridge into Cambridge, all the worry she felt for Danny spilled out of her in a loud stream of curses, and Audrey pounded on the steering wheel.

I had him, and I couldn't do it! she thought. *I couldn't pull the trigger!*

Jenna's eyes were red and raw as she slumped in a chair in the hospital waiting room. She looked up expectantly when she heard footsteps approaching and through her tears saw Audrey Gaines walking over to her. Dr. Slikowski had been waiting with her for the past two hours, and in that time, although they had spoken little, she had calmed down at least a bit. A fresh torrent of emotions rushed through her when she stood up. She was trembling as she embraced the woman and held on to her tightly, almost desperately.

"He . . . ," Jenna started to say, but her voice choked off, and she was unable to do anything but cling to Audrey, grateful for the strength and support she felt coming from her. The bond she felt between them was instant and immediate. Without saying a word, she knew that they shared something special—their concern for Danny.

Before they could speak, more footsteps signaled the arrival of a young, dark-haired doctor Jenna had not seen before. The man went right to Audrey, and it was clear that she must have spoken to him about Danny earlier in the day.

"Dr. Skillings," Audrey said immediately. "How is he?"

The doctor pondered the question as though he had not expected it. "Well, Detective Mariano's condition has stabilized. However, he remains unconscious. We believe that he may have suffered a minor concussion, hit his head on something beneath the snow perhaps, or been struck. We're unable to determine that at this time.

"As to his condition: He suffered first-degree burns ranging in severity over a large portion of his body. Eighteen percent of his body surface—in this case his front upper torso, the chest and abdominal areas—suffered second- and third-degree burns. The third-degree burns seem to be localized in one area on his abdomen, and will very likely become infected. Skin grafts are almost a certainty at this point, if he survives."

Jenna shuddered and wrapped her arms around herself, unable to warm the chill that seemed to have settled into her bones. She glanced at Slick and Audrey, then at Doctor Skillings again.

"*If* he survives?" she repeated, staring at the doctor.

"If he had not dived into the snow immediately, he surely would have died already," Dr. Skillings said. "As it is, the burns he received are quite serious, but not as bad as they might have been."

"What's the prognosis?" Dr. Slikowski asked, rolling his chair closer to the doctor.

"Our burn specialist, Doctor Palcovich, and his team have assessed the burns, but of course it will be a couple of weeks at least before we could graft,"

Skillings said. Jenna noticed that he assumed a more professional tone when talking to Slick. "We've intubated, though there do not seem to be any signs of smoke inhalation or lung damage. He's on a central line and a ventilator, of course, but so far we haven't had to do eschars."

"What's that?" Jenna asked quickly. It was an ugly-sounding word.

Dr. Skillings looked at her doubtfully, as though he would rather not tell her. Slick, however, did not hesitate for a moment.

"In the area where Danny has third-degree burns, the skin is practically nonexistent. What is there now is essentially a sort of encasement, and it will tighten across the burn area. If there's a danger that it will negatively impact his breathing or circulation, they'll have to make deep cuts in the burn area to release that pressure. If they have to do that, the grafts would be more significant later, and the chances of infection are greatly increased."

"But they didn't have to do that, so that's good, right?" Jenna asked.

"That's good," Slick confirmed, and smiled gently.

Audrey stood beside Jenna and slipped an arm around her.

"Will he be scarred?" Audrey asked.

Skillings shifted uncomfortably. "Well, once again, this is all predicated on his returning to consciousness within the next twenty-four hours or so. If he doesn't, there are far greater complications to consider. But best case scenario? There will be some scarring.

That's unavoidable. At this point, Doctor Palcovich believes that the only graft will be the abdominal area—barring any unforeseen damage from infection—and that means minimal scarring in other areas of his chest and neck, and the change in skin texture left behind from the graft on his abdomen."

Slick nodded knowingly as Doctor Skillings paused and took a deep breath. The professional facade dropped immediately when he turned to focus once again on Jenna and Audrey.

"The next twenty-four hours are going to be critical," Dr. Skillings said, his voice low and sympathetic. "If we continue to see no sign of respiratory difficulty, he'll be taken off the ventilator. That's good. What you must remember is that the human skin is an organ, and that organ has suffered horrible trauma. Still, though the recovery will take time, if he regains consciousness soon, then we are confident that he'll be okay."

And if he doesn't? Jenna thought.

But she already knew the answer.

chapter 12

Danny was all over the news. *Decorated Somerset homicide detective burned in an incident similar to a series of recent deaths in the area.* Jenna hadn't even been aware that Danny was "decorated" and didn't know for what, but the moment of wonder that bit of news inspired was just that: a moment. She had turned the television on out of a morbid, almost hypnotic curiosity that she did not quite understand, flipped channels for all of seven minutes, and then shut it off with a shudder.

Jenna paced. She had a quiz on the heart in Gross Anatomy and a test in European history the next day and she knew she should be studying. She just couldn't.

Yoshiko and Hunter sat on the top bunk, legs dangling over the side, and watched her with expressions of both sympathy and bewilderment. It was after six o'clock, and neither one of them had made any move to leave—not even to go to the bathroom—since Jenna had come back from Somerset Medical Center around four and broken the news to them. They had hugged her, held her, let her cry, then tried to tell her everything would be all right.

Jenna had snapped, just a little, though she knew they were just trying to help. Since then, they had just sat up there on the bunk and watched her helplessly.

She paced.

With a pained sigh, Yoshiko slipped off the top bunk and moved into her path. Jenna stopped in the middle of the room and gazed up at her, facing off with the girl who was the closest thing she had to a best friend.

"Jenna." Yoshiko pressed her lips together and stared at her, as though trying to communicate some telepathic message that Jenna just wasn't capable of hearing.

"What am I supposed to do?" Jenna demanded suddenly.

Yoshiko flinched and Jenna reached around to grab the back of her head, then gently leaned her own forehead against her roommate's. "Jesus, Yoshiko, what am I supposed to do?"

Slowly, Yoshiko slipped her hand behind Jenna's neck and laid the other comfortingly on her shoulder and they just stood there a moment. Jenna felt as though her friend were taking on some of her pain somehow, sharing the burden, and it made her want to cry again to feel how much Yoshiko cared.

"I'm so sorry, Jenna," she said. Then she pulled her

head back so she could stare into Jenna's eyes and slid her hand down so that she was now holding on to both of Jenna's shoulders tightly. "There's nothing you can do except find a way to occupy your mind until you get some kind of word from Slick or Audrey."

"That's not good enough," Jenna said, hating the crack in her voice. "I can't concentrate on studying, I can't just sit and watch TV or read. I can't not think about him. I know you think I'm crazy to think something could happen between us, but even if it didn't, that wouldn't change the fact that I care about him. A lot. It'd be the same if something happened to you or Hunter."

Jenna threw her hands up, ran them through her hair, and turned to pace back toward the windows.

"Do you want us to get out of here?" Yoshiko asked. "I mean, would you rather be alone?"

Automatically, Jenna began to shake her head. But as the question sank in, she stopped herself. Finally she looked at them. "I don't want you to go far," she said, "but maybe I could use just a little time to myself, even just to curl up in a ball and hide. Is that okay?"

"More than okay," Yoshiko said. "We'll go and study in the common area for a little while."

Hunter slid down off Yoshiko's bunk, walked over and kissed Jenna on top of her head. "If you need us, we'll be right there."

Jenna nodded, feeling a bit guilty. "Thanks, you guys. I don't know what I'd do without you." Her words sank in quickly, made her think of Danny and also of Melody, and her stomach churned.

"And I don't ever want to find out," she added.

Not two minutes after they had left her and Jenna was curled up in a fetal position on her bed, the phone rang. She ignored it, afraid of what news it would bring, and listened instead for the answering machine to pick up. The volume was on low, specifically so they could screen calls if they did not feel like answering.

"Jenna, hi. It's Mom."

She frowned and glanced at the phone on the wall.

"I . . . I just saw a report about your detective friend on the news. I know you must be really worried and I wanted to check on you. 'Cause *I'm* worried about *you*. Please call to let me know you're okay. I love you, honey."

There was a soft beep and the clicking sound as the machine reset itself for another incoming call. Jenna felt bad that she had not answered, but she was only just beginning to get hold of herself and her emotions, and if she tried to tell her mother how she felt, it would tear her open again. She knew that.

So she just lay there with her mother's voice echoing in her head.

And her own voice as well. *What am I supposed to do?* The words came back to her again and again until finally, she sat up in the bed and stared at the phone.

"Something," she whispered.

Anything but lie here and be afraid for him.

She went to the phone and called Slick at his home

number, surprised that she remembered it. It wasn't every day that she called him at home. On the third ring, a female voice answered. Natalie Kerchak, Slick's girlfriend.

"Natalie, it's Jenna."

"Jenna, God, are you all right? Walter told me what had happened to your friend and—"

"I'm as all right as I can be, I guess," Jenna replied, interrupting. "Listen, is Dr. Slikowski there?"

Natalie paused before answering. "Actually, no, he's not. I made dinner for both of us, and he did come home, but he was pretty fidgety. I knew he wanted to go back to the office. I told him to go. Most of the time I'd kill him for ruining a dinner date like that, but . . . anyway, he left about twenty minutes ago. Do you want to leave him a message?"

"No thanks," Jenna said quickly. "I think I'm going over there myself."

"I thought you might," Natalie replied. "Tell him I'll keep the rest of his dinner warm for him."

Once again there was no music playing in Slick's office when Jenna arrived. She crossed the outer office area where her cubicle was and stood in the doorway looking in at him. Slick was so engrossed in his work that he had not heard her enter. The Nash, Sobler, and Dahms files were spread all over the office. Jenna could not see any of those names from her position at the door, but she knew that those were the files he was studying. She knew it from the profoundly troubled expression on his face, and the lack of music.

She had a sudden and completely abstract fear that she would never hear jazz in this office again, and brushed it off.

"Hey," she said softly.

Slick started in his wheelchair, dropped the photograph he was holding, and looked up at her in surprise.

"Lord, Jenna, don't sneak up on me like that," Slick snapped.

"No sneaking," she promised. "Natalie told me you were here. She said she's keeping dinner warm for you. Was that some kind of innuendo that I missed?"

The M.E. blinked in obvious astonishment at her joke, and Jenna chuckled to herself, put a hand up to her mouth to hide her smile, and blushed a bit.

"That was awful. I'm sorry."

"No, no," Slick said, waving away her apology. "Just not used to that sort of humor from you."

"Anything to get my mind off Danny, I guess."

Their eyes met, but both of them studiously avoided looking at the files spread about the room. Almost simultaneously, both of them stopped smiling.

"It's not really working, I've gotta say," Jenna confessed. "You're down here working on the burnings."

"I can't get them out of my head."

"Me either," Jenna told him. "I thought I might be able to help."

Slick nodded, eyes narrowed. "I'm sure you can. Your perspective is always fresh, Jenna. I need that right now because I can't find a thing in these files that's going to help the police catch this man, or even to explain how he does what he does."

Jenna walked to the desk and picked up the photograph Slick had dropped. Kendall Sobler's corpse on the street outside State Street T Station, the soles of her sneakers melted onto the tar. She nibbled on her lower lip for a moment, and sat down across from him.

"Pyrokinesis," she said, voice firm. "We've toyed with the idea, kind of implied that it's what we think, established that it's the only thing that fits the facts, but we've never really said it for sure."

"Because we can't *be* sure," Slick reminded her. "It's never been proven to exist. And we have no witnesses to confirm it."

"We have Danny."

Slick raised an eyebrow. "Danny is still unconscious."

Jenna nodded. "But he would never have let this guy get close enough to burn him any other way. Especially not there in front of his place. I mean— okay, if you set up some kind of . . . incendiary or whatever in his apartment or his car, but not like this."

She watched Slick expectantly. After a moment's contemplation, he raised his eyebrows and sat back in his wheelchair.

"All right. Let's say we proceed from that assumption. What do we gain by it?" Slick asked. "The police need to be able to prove it in order to charge Victor

Frost. First we'd have to figure out how to convince them, and then we'd have to link Frost to those murders."

Jenna took a deep breath and let it out slowly. "Well, I'm not going to antagonize Frost and have someone videotape it."

They sat for a few moments in silence. At length, Jenna looked back up at Slick. "I hate to say this, but maybe the best we can do is find a way to convince them that this is what they're dealing with, and maybe help figure out a way to confront Frost without anyone else getting hurt."

"We're talking about surfing the 'net again, aren't we?" Slick asked.

Jenna nodded and chuckled indulgently.

Slick smiled. "It's a tall order. But let's see what we can do. Before I can convince anybody else, I've got to convince myself any of this is even possible."

Jenna went into the outer office and booted up the computer at her desk. As she logged on, Dr. Slikowski rolled his chair up beside her. Only a few minutes into their Web search, Jenna hissed under her breath.

"Whoa," she said.

"I had no idea there would be so much information," Slick commented.

"Yeah," Jenna agreed. "But now we have to sift through it all for the stuff that sounds remotely plausible."

A little more than two hours later—time in which Jenna tried and failed to forget that Danny still lay unconscious two floors above them—they had found some startling cases. Many were spontaneous human combustion situations. Most authorities discounted its existence, but those staid doctors and scientists were hard pressed to explain certain incidents. They were able to reconfirm a dozen times over that none of the three victims—*four, counting Danny*, Jenna thought—had experienced SHC. That entailed people bursting into flame, but all those incidents were characterized by the victims being burned from the inside out, not by an external source.

But the SHC stuff was only a small part of the story.

Pyrokinesis had a long history, including some disturbing recent precedents. In 1982 a little boy in Formia, Italy, was sitting in a dentist's waiting room when the comic book he was reading inexplicably burst into flames. Other instances soon followed, with dozens of incidents where the boy, Benedetto Supino, brushed by a piece of furniture or other household object only to have it blaze with fire. Several times he awoke to find his bedsheets on fire, and yet with no harm to himself. Doctors in Rome could find no explanation and no physical abnormality in the boy.

Similar stories abounded—from 1891 in Canada to 1986 in the Ukraine. In 1983, a Scottish nanny named Carol Compton had actually been put on trial in Italy for arson and attempted murder—by fire, of course—of her three-year-old charge. All of those fires, the authorities claimed, had been set by the woman with the power of her mind alone. The Italian government obviously believed in pyrokinesis.

"Fascinating," Slick muttered as he leaned over beside her, the two of them sharing the computer monitor.

"No kidding," Jenna replied. Then she looked at him. Something in his tone drew her attention. "You don't just mean the pyrokinesis stuff, do you?"

Slick was thoughtful and sat back in his wheelchair. "That, certainly. But there's a distinction here I find interesting. If we are inclined to side with the believers here rather than the skeptics—which I think we've already decided we must given the preponderance of evidence in this case—there seem to be two main types of pyrokinesis. First there are those, like the Brough boy in California, who can start a fire with a glance. His power is purely mental. Then there are others, like that Italian boy, for whom contact seems necessary. Let's call it tactile pyrokinesis."

Jenna's mind flashed back to the scorch marks on the victims' clothing and the burned handprints on both sides of Matthew Dahms's head. "Victor Frost is a tactile pyrokinetic," she said. "The touching is part of it. He can't burn you if he can't touch you."

"Or if he can't concentrate or focus on you," Slick replied. "At least, hypothetically. If he were unconscious, for instance, or drugged. He might burn his bedsheets like a child unable to control his bladder during sleep, but he could not focus an attack."

Jenna stared at him, an idea forming in her head. "And if, let's say, someone were to inject him with something, like sodium pentothal or even plain old morphine, something that knocked him for a loop, he might have a hard time directing his power, and he also might reveal its existence by accident."

Slick swallowed hard. He removed his glasses and rubbed the bridge of his nose, then held the spectacles in his lap a moment as he gazed blearily around the room.

"You realize," he said tentatively, without looking at Jenna, "that what you're talking about could cost Detective Gaines her job? That without Frost's consent—something he would never give if he is the killer and all of this is true—it would be a violation of his civil rights to introduce such a chemical into his body by force or any other means."

"Only if Frost knew Audrey did it. And don't tell me you think she'd hesitate for a second, after what this guy did to Danny."

He stared at her. Eventually, he gave a tiny shrug and a sigh. "I can't believe we're having this conversation," he said. "Not just about Audrey, but about this in general. I have seen some extraordinary things over the years, some more outlandish than this, but I have never dealt with something so obviously possible that was so completely dismissed by those in authority."

"They just don't read Sherlock Holmes," Jenna told him.

Slick chuckled.

"Once you've eliminated the impossible . . . ," Jenna began.

"Whatever remains, no matter how improbable, must be the truth," Slick finished for her. "I suspect

Audrey's up in Danny's room right now. Do you want to tell her, or shall I?"

Jenna reached out and laid a hand over his. "You go home and finish the dinner Natalie made for you. I hope she hasn't already gone home, or you'll really be in the doghouse."

"Actually," Slick said, a bit off-handedly, "she is home. Natalie moved in last week."

Jenna's eyes went wide. "Wow," she said. Then she laughed softly, both happy for Slick and surprised that he had chosen to share that with her. "That . . . that's great. At least somebody has something good happening."

Danny was a wreck. Audrey sat in a hard wooden chair next to his bed in the intensive care unit and studied his face. That was good, actually, because, looking at his face, Danny didn't look that bad. He was burned, sure. His eyebrows were gone and his skin was bright red as if he'd fallen asleep in the sun for about a day and a half. But Audrey wouldn't even look at the rest of him. She couldn't. There were dressings on the third-degree burn area on his abdomen, but his chest was covered with red, raw areas where it looked as though the skin had been peeled away.

"Oh, Jesus, Danny," she whispered.

Audrey wanted to reach out and hold his hand, but she was afraid to hurt him, to touch him. Though his chest and abdomen got the worst of it, his whole body was burned. Most of his hair had been incinerated.

"Wake up," she told him, her low voice almost angry. "The doc says as long as you wake up soon, you'll probably be okay. Take a while, sure, some rehab, maybe a graft on your belly there, but you'll be okay. You just have to wake up."

Teeth gritted, she leaned in toward him and her voice dropped even below a whisper. "And when you do wake up, you can ID Frost as the killer, and we can *nail* the son of a bitch."

Danny moaned a bit, almost as though he understood, but he didn't wake up. Audrey sat back in the chair and just watched him, her eyes growing heavy. She was exhausted after the day she'd had, starting with almost no sleep the night before and the early morning visit from Lieutenant Gonci. If it weren't for the hard chair, she would have drifted off to sleep easily by now. As it was, her eyelids were drooping when a white nurse came in to check on the dressings on Danny's abdominal wounds.

"I'm sorry. I didn't know anyone was here," the nurse said.

But she didn't sound sorry. In fact, Audrey thought she sounded a bit edgy, considering that she was talking to someone who was visiting a patient in ICU.

"Don't mind me. Just do what you need to do," Audrey told her.

The nurse eyed her carefully. "Only family is allowed in the ICU."

Audrey stood and stared at the woman. Slowly, she pulled her badge out of her pocket and hung it in front of the nurse's eyes. "I'm the closest thing in the world this man has to a family. I am going to be here with him around the clock. You have a problem with that?"

With a bitter pout, the woman glanced away. "Just doing my job, officer."

"Detective," Audrey snapped. "Detective Audrey Gaines. And your job is to take care of my partner. Okay?"

The nurse nodded.

"Oh, and do me a favor? See if you can get an orderly to bring me something more comfortable to sit in. Something I can sleep in."

"I'll see what I can do," the nurse replied coldly.

A short while later a large orderly carried a chair that was almost as large as he was out of the waiting area and into the ICU. Audrey slipped into it gratefully, even smiled at the expressionless orderly, and not ten minutes after he had gone, she fell deeply asleep to the lulling rhythm of Danny's ventilator.

chapter 13

Jenna was filled with nervous anticipation as she rode the elevator up to the burn unit on the fourth floor. Concern for Danny still dominated her mind and filled her with sadness, but she was also happy that—finally—she was *doing* something to help. Though there had been a number of mysteries involved in this case, she had not pursued it any further than the normal limits of her job because the police seemed to have a handle on it. Danny suspected someone, and the state police had formed a task force. Slick had told them they should at least consider the possibility of pyrokinesis.

Jenna had done all that she could have. But with Danny so badly injured, she could not help but wonder if that was true or if she could somehow have prevented his injuries.

A bell sounded as the fourth-floor light came on, and the elevator slowed to a stop. As soon as the doors slid open, Jenna stepped out and started down the hallway to the nurses' station in the ICU. It was late and the only person at the central desk was a thin, red-headed woman who looked up, startled, as Jenna approached the chest-high counter. The only other person in sight was a shortish guy wearing blue hospital scrubs who was mopping the hall floor.

"May I help you?" the nurse asked. Her voice was low and flat, almost a whisper, and there was something in her eyes that told Jenna that she was having a rough night and wouldn't appreciate anyone's adding to her burden.

"Yes, hi," Jenna said, smiling pleasantly as she held out her hand for the nurse to shake. She noticed the nurse's name badge: Rebecca Sands. "My name's Jenna Blake. I work with Dr. Slikowski downstairs. You have a patient here in the burn unit. Danny Mariano."

Nurse Sands sighed heavily and glanced up at the ceiling for a moment. Then she regarded Jenna coolly. "Dr. Slikowski is the medical examiner. Mr. Mariano is still alive."

Jenna flinched, taken aback a bit by the woman's manner. "I, uh, I just need a moment."

"You're not a doctor, Miss Blake. Unless you're a member of the immediate family, I can't allow you in to see him."

"Oh, I realize that," Jenna said brightly, not wanting to push hospital protocol. "Actually, it's Detective Gaines I need to see. Do you know if she's still in there?"

Instantly, the expression on the nurse's face went sour. She pursed her lips together so tightly they turned white, and her neck and jaw muscles visibly tightened.

"Yes, she's in there," Nurse Sands replied, her voice filled with a tension that bordered on outright hostility.

Jenna began to understand the nurse's attitude. When it came to making sure Danny was being properly taken care of, Audrey would no doubt be more than demanding. Chances are she had gotten on more than a few of the nurse's nerves.

But Jenna could not let that stop her.

"Look, I'm sorry to bother you," she said, with as much sincerity as she could muster, "but I have a very important message for Detective Gaines from Dr. Slikowski." She folded her hands together and smiled as she leaned forward on the desk, all sweetness and light. "Would it be possible for you to let Detective Gaines know that I'm here?"

Nurse Sands regarded her silently for a moment or two as she considered the request. She was obviously torn, but just when she seemed about to relent, her expression hardened again. The look on her face was a mixture of anger and fear as she glanced over her shoulder at one of the closed doors on the opposite side of the hall. Jenna followed her gaze, knowing that was Danny's room. The man washing the floors had paused to regard them, but when the nurse glared at him, he immediately set to work again, moving his mop across the floor with wide, careless strokes. The mop made a rough, scraping sound on the floor.

"Do you know Detective Gaines?" Nurse Sands finally asked. "Are you a friend of hers?"

"Yes. We've worked together in the past," Jenna said, nodding eagerly and hoping that her easygoing tactic was going to work.

"Well," Nurse Sands continued, her voice hardening even more, "the detective is asleep in there right now, and unless you think I look like someone who enjoys poking sticks into a bear cage, I don't think I'm going to disturb her."

Jenna was crestfallen. What she had to tell Audrey was vitally important, not just to the case, but to her and Danny's safety as well. Even if the state-run task force had figured out what was going on and were acting on it, Jenna wanted to make sure Audrey knew what she was up against. She and Slick had figured out how they might combat the killer if they could get close enough to him. Audrey needed to know.

"I'm sure Detective Gaines won't mind if you tell her it's me," Jenna said, unable to keep the pleading tone out of her voice.

Nurse Sands eyed Jenna and seemed once again about to give in, but then she shivered slightly and shook her head. "I'm sure the detective has a message service or a beeper or cell phone. You can reach her one of those ways. For both of us, I think it would be better just to let her sleep for now."

Jenna knew that she was not going to get anywhere. She stared past the nurse at the closed door and thought of Danny. Nurse Sands was right. She could reach Audrey any number of ways. But she had relished the possibility that she might be able to see Danny, however briefly, and no matter how bad off he was. But she knew she should not force the issue. Nurse Sands would call security, and she'd be thrown out. The last thing she needed was to make a scene.

"Could I leave a note for you to give her when she wakes up, then?" Jenna asked.

Nurse Sands looked at her, resigned, and nodded once. Without saying another word, she handed her a pad of paper and a pen. Jenna thought for a moment about what to write, then simply scrawled:

> *Audrey—*
> *We know how to fight him. Please be careful. Call me or Dr. S. as soon as you can.*
> *—Jenna*

She folded the paper in half, then wrote "Detective Gaines" on the front, underlined it twice, and handed it back to Nurse Sands.

"Please make sure she gets it," Jenna said. "It's very important."

"I will . . . once she wakes up," Nurse Sands said with a curt nod that told Jenna she was dismissed.

Tired and worried, Jenna thanked the nurse and turned to go. She couldn't resist one final, longing glance at the closed door of the ICU, behind which

Danny was fighting for his life. If he did not regain consciousness soon . . .

Jenna bit her lip, then whispered a soft prayer and willed all of her strength to Danny. Even as she did so, though, she had the odd sensation that something else was wrong. She couldn't put a finger on it, but something seemed odd . . . out of place. As she walked down the hallway to the elevator and pressed the button for the ground floor, she tried to ignore it. But she could not shake the nagging thought that something was wrong.

Let it go, she told herself, closing her eyes and leaning against the wall as she waited for the elevator to arrive. *You're just worried about Danny.*

As true as that was, though, she couldn't deny that there was something else, some tiny little undefined *something* teasing at the back of her mind. It wasn't just her concern for Danny. It was something else, something small and inconsequential, like a single piece of a jigsaw puzzle that doesn't quite fit. Another day she might have ignored it, but now that it was bugging her, Jenna knew that she wasn't going to let it go until she figured out what it was.

The elevator arrived, the bell making a soft *bing* as the doors rattled open. Jenna stepped inside and pressed the button for the ground floor. Throughout the ride down, the sensation that something was out of place only grew stronger. It burrowed into her mind like a thorn.

In her mind, she ran through her encounter with Nurse Sands, trying to pin down exactly what was bothering her. Jenna buttoned her coat, slipped on her gloves, and wrapped her scarf around her neck, then she stepped out into the cold night, shivering as she started up the hill toward Sparrow Hall.

It was late, but she did not know if she would be able to sleep. Not until she knew Danny had woken up and would recover. But she would have to try. She had to be up early for classes. Maybe she'd even give Roseanne a call to see if she was up for a power walk before breakfast. She had responsibilities she could not ignore, and that meant she could not simply drop them. The doctors were doing everything they could for Danny, and Audrey was right there beside him. He couldn't be in better hands.

So why was she still worried?

Jenna crossed Carpenter Street in front of Keates Hall and was just making her way around the side of the building when it hit her.

The mop.

The janitor had stopped mopping the floor while Jenna spoke to the nurse, almost as though he were listening . . . as if he had an interest in what she had to say. That might have been simple nosiness. *But what about the mop?*

In the back of her mind, she could hear again the sound of the mop hitting the floor, the scrape as the janitor swirled it across the tile. She could picture the bucket up against a nearby wall. *The mop. Clack, scrape.* The sound of it resonated in her head.

The mop was dry.

*   *   *

As she dozed, Audrey was still aware in some distant, dreamy way of the sounds of the hospital all around her. She faded in and out, lulled by the steady beep of monitors, the faint hissing of the respirator, and the soft sound of whispered voices and feet, scuffing by in the corridor.

The doorknob clicked. Instantly alert, she sat up and looked over to see the door edge open.

Maybe it was a nurse, trying to be polite. *Maybe.* But Audrey had not stuck by Danny's side only so he would have company while he recovered. She was there in case Frost decided to finish the job.

Moving slowly, she shifted her hand down to her service revolver, released the strap, and drew it. She had turned the lights down in the room so she could sleep, but even in silhouette, even through the plastic curtains around Danny's bed, she recognized Victor Frost as he slipped into the room. He glanced back out into the hallway once to make sure he was clear before easing the door shut behind him.

Audrey shifted forward quickly in her chair and stood up, her service weapon aimed straight at him.

"Hold it right there," she said, her voice low and harsh with command.

In the dim light of the room, she could see the twisted smirk on his face as he slowly turned to face her.

"Hmm . . . not a very sound sleeper, I see," Frost said.

"I thought you might show up," Audrey said with a snarl.

This is it. My second chance. She could shoot him right there on the spot and claim he had attacked her when he came into the room to finish off Danny. It would be easy to substantiate since he was wearing a hospital uniform and obviously had no business being in the ICU this late at night.

But Audrey hesitated. Not out of fear, but because she was concerned about discharging her firearm in the ICU.

"You don't want to give me a reason." Audrey steadied her aim as she moved toward her purse. Her cellular phone was inside. And on the small table beside Danny's bed was the little plastic button she could press to call a nurse.

"You move a muscle, and I swear I'll shoot," she vowed.

"Well, then, I guess you've got me." Frost chuckled as he raised his arms above his head.

Audrey reached quickly into her purse and punched in the memory buttons that would automatically dial the Somerset police station, eyes on Frost. In the dim light of the room, Audrey found it difficult to see clearly. As she waited for the call to be put through, Frost made his move.

He darted to one side and dragged his right hand across the wall. Instantly, a blazing line of fire burst out of the plaster, flaring brightly enough to leave a blinding afterimage streaking across Audrey's vision before burning out. A cloying, smoky smell filled the room.

She squinted and swung her revolver around, trying to track him. Just before she squeezed the trigger, she realized that he was too close to the oxygen tanks by the wall. If she hit one of them with a bullet, the whole room might explode.

Then it was too late.

Frost was on her. He grabbed her gun with his right hand and tried to twist it from her grip. She held on.

"You're fast, I'll give you that," he said, spitting the words through gritted teeth. His breath was hot and stale. "But not quite fast enough."

As he continued to try to wrest the gun from her grip, Audrey felt a sudden, intense heat blossom in her palm. Within seconds, it felt like she had stuck her hand inside a raging furnace.

With a single, swift motion, she yanked her gun up and to one side, wrenching his arm, then punched him hard in the armpit. Frost grunted with pain and his arm went slack and Audrey jerked her gun away, staggering steps back, desperate to avoid his touch.

Her hand stung from the intense heat as she tried to raise her revolver to shoot him, but the gun was too hot to hold. She glanced at it and saw that the metal was glowing a bright, cherry red and had started to melt. Howling with pain, she dropped the weapon to the floor.

Oh God, it's true, Audrey thought. *It's all true.*

Frost smiled at her, cruel and cold. "You know what they say. If you can't stand the heat, get out of the kitchen," he sneered. "You're not going to win this one, Detective Gaines." He took a few measured steps closer to her, cocked his head to one side and studied her a moment. "But you know, I kind of like you, so I think I'll let you live another minute or two."

Frost turned on Danny, who still lay unconscious on the bed. For a moment or two, his expression was unreadable, but then he frowned and shook his head sadly.

"I hate to say it, but it looks like you tried to lie to me," he said, casting a menacing glance at Audrey. "He never came to, did he? He couldn't have identified me."

Audrey trembled with rage, but did not dare to attack him. If she tried to fight him hand to hand, he would incinerate her.

"What are you going to do, Frost? Kill us? Then what? You don't think the hospital has security cameras? They've already got you on film. Your only chance is to run now, fast and far." She had to fight hard to keep her voice steady, but it was more out of anger than fear.

Frost snorted with laughter. A dull, angry fire lit his eyes as he stared her down. Very slowly, like the lingering touch of a lover, he ran his forefinger along the metal bar at the foot of Danny's bed. Instantly, the metal began to glow and crackle. Thin wisps of blue smoke rose up.

"It's over, Frost," Audrey said softly.

"Yes, it is," Frost replied as he moved to the head of the bed, his hands raised above Danny's unconscious form. "It is most *definitely* over."

*   *   *

"He's in there!"

The words burst from Jenna as she exited the elevator and ran toward the ICU nurses' station. Nurse Sands was still alone at the desk, doing some paperwork. The janitor was nowhere in sight.

Startled, Nurse Sands looked up at Jenna. "Hold it!" she shouted. "You can't go in there!"

But Jenna was already past her. She pushed open the door to Danny's room and all of her worst fears were realized. Audrey stood in the far corner, angry and defiant, gripping her right hand to her chest as though she'd been hurt. Beside Danny's bed, the man who had posed as a janitor turned menacingly toward Jenna and Nurse Sands.

"Company," the man said, his face split by a wide grin. "I just love company. Who's up for a cookout?"

"What are you doing in this room?" Nurse Sands demanded. "This patient is in critical condition."

"Call security! Right *now!*" Audrey shouted. "He's a killer!"

Nurse Sands turned to run from the room, but the man lunged at her, grabbed her from behind and started to choke her. She struggled valiantly, her legs kicking so wildly that one of her white sneakers flipped off, but he easily overpowered her.

Jenna started to rush him, but then she saw a long streak of charred plaster on the wall, and thought of his hands. His touch. In that moment of her hesitation, he lifted the nurse clear off the floor and threw her toward Audrey. A heartbeat after he let her go,

Nurse Sands burst into flames, a ball of orange fire erupting all around her, engulfing her. She landed in a shrieking, flailing tumble on the floor in front of Audrey and screamed in agony as the raging fire swept over her.

Jenna was frozen with horror and astonishment, but Audrey reacted quickly. She grabbed a large vase of flowers off a small table near Danny's bed and threw water onto the writhing woman. The pyrokinetic started toward them even as Audrey grabbed a blanket and fell upon Nurse Sands, smothering the flames.

The killer's back was to Jenna, and she knew that she had to act fast. Without a backward glance she bolted from the room. Behind the nurses' station was a glass-fronted emergency medical cabinet. She still wore her gloves from being outside, so she made a fist and punched the glass.

Jenna's hands trembled as she rifled through the contents of the cabinet. Plenty of syringes, but where . . . *here!* She pulled out a glass ampoule of morphine, snapped off the top, then filled the syringe with the drug. It seemed to take forever. She could still hear Nurse Sands screaming back in Danny's room. A couple of nurses appeared in the corridor, and an orderly as well.

Got it, Jenna thought.

She stood up and headed for the door to Danny's room.

"Hey!" one of the nurses called to her. "What do you think you're—"

"Call security," Jenna told her, voice barely above a whisper so there was no chance the killer might hear her. "Call the police. Tell them there's an officer down."

Jenna took a deep breath outside the room, then slipped inside. The killer stood over Audrey and Nurse Sands, who lay writhing on the floor, her face a bubbling mess of seared flesh.

"Keep away from her, Frost," Audrey warned. "I'm not going to let you kill anyone else."

"That's actually pretty funny," Frost replied, his voice a deep, threatening rumble.

Everything Jenna knew about giving an injection she had learned from watching her friend Marielle Kent give herself insulin injections for diabetes back in junior high. That and television. But she didn't have time to learn to do it the right way.

Jenna rushed him. She raised the needle in her clenched fist like she was going to stab him with a knife, thumb on the tip of the plunger, then jabbed it into his back in the meat of his shoulder muscle. Frost jumped and let out a wild howl of pain and rage, but Jenna managed to depress the plunger with her thumb before he wheeled around and swung at her. She managed to duck the blow and darted away.

"*Dammit, that hurt!*" the man wailed as he reached behind his back and yanked the needle out. He threw it against the wall, then came at her, his hands outstretched.

The orderly came in from the hall. Two of the nurses looked on behind him.

"Hold on, buddy," the orderly said. "Security's on the way. Don't make another move."

Frost turned to the orderly with a savage, bestial snarl. He reached for the man. The orderly grabbed his arm, ducked behind him and got him into a chokehold.

"Don't let him touch you!" Audrey cried as she tried to rise to help the orderly with Frost.

Nurse Sands rasped out a pained shout and grabbed Audrey's jacket, held on so tight that Audrey stumbled and fell to her knees again beside the burned woman.

The killer reached up with his free hand and touched the orderly's forearm. Flesh started to burn. The orderly cried out, let go of Frost, and staggered backward, beating at the fire on his arm.

But the flames did not spread.

Frost lunged for Jenna again. She tried to run out of the room but the nurses stood there gawking, making themselves both targets for the killer and obstacles to Jenna's escape. One of them had started to shout as soon as the orderly's arm began to burn, but there was still no sign of security or the police.

"Out of the way!" Jenna screamed at them, and used both hands to shove them back as she fled into the corridor.

"Not so fast, girlie," Frost shouted from behind her, but he had begun to slur his words. As she burst out into the hall, she felt his hand brush against her back and snag her jacket, but she tore away from him.

Frost burst out of Danny's ICU room, but as he came toward her, Jenna saw that his steps were a little wobbly. His gaze was glassy, and he blinked several times and swayed on his feet.

Frost stopped, in a daze, and looked at his hands, then at Jenna. "What did you do to me?"

Before Jenna could answer, Audrey burst out of Danny's room and rammed an elbow against the back of Frost's head. The killer went sprawling across the tiles, skull bouncing off the floor.

"Get in there!" Audrey snapped at the nurses who were standing, wide-eyed, in the hallway.

As they ran into Danny's room to help Nurse Sands and the orderly and to check on Danny, Audrey turned warily toward Frost.

"What *did* you do to him?" Audrey asked, never taking her eyes off the killer.

"Morphine," Jenna said quickly. "He can only burn by touch, and even then, he's got to be able to focus to do it. Keep him drugged, keep away from his hands, and you should be all right."

Audrey shot her a look of startled admiration. "Remind me never to get in a scrape with you, all right?"

Frost started to turn over, moaning. His eyes were even more glassy. Audrey used her foot to push him back over on his stomach, then yanked his arms up and cuffed him.

"Is Danny all right?" Jenna asked, afraid to hear the answer.

"Frost never touched him," Audrey assured her. "But he's still unconscious. And that nurse needs immediate medical attention."

With a sudden clatter of doors slamming open and shouts of alarm, security and police personnel burst in from the emergency exit doors on either side of the hallway. Audrey was helping Jenna up as they swarmed around. Several people asked her questions at once, but Jenna wasn't listening.

Danny's okay.

═══════════════
═══════════════
═══════════════
═══════════════
═══════════════
═══════════════

e p i l o g u e

When Jenna woke up the next day, the sky was gray but it had begun to warm up considerably. The windows were open several inches and fresh air blew in, helping to clear the fog from her brain. Jenna glanced over at her clock and was stunned to find that it was nearly noon.

"Oh, no," she moaned softly.

Her mind was so numb, her body so exhausted, that she could not even remember what day it was. All she knew was, wherever she was supposed to be at the moment, she was still in her bed instead. With a deep sigh, Jenna let her eyes close again. She felt so drained that it seemed a chore just to get up.

Danny!

Suddenly she was up, out of bed, scrambling around the room for her robe and the basket of shampoo and things she took with her to the girls' shower. The phone had not rung and that was a bad sign, but by now the doctors would have a prognosis on Danny, and she wanted to get over to the medical center to look in on him.

Wrapped in her robe, a towel over her shoulder and the wire basket in hand, she opened the door and stepped into the hall.

"I thought you were going to sleep all day."

Jenna turned to see Yoshiko sitting in a chair down the hall. She had a textbook in her hands and an open notebook on her lap, but her chair was pulled out into the middle of the common area so that she could keep an eye on the door to their room.

"Hey," Jenna said. "You playing guardian angel?"

"Someone has to," Yoshiko told her.

Jenna nodded, smiled in appreciation, and walked toward her. "I'm going to take a quick shower, then go over to check in on Danny."

Yoshiko grinned. "He's awake."

"What?" Jenna gasped. She stared at Yoshiko, heart starting to pound in her chest. All the pain and the fear for him that she had been trying to keep rein over dissipated instantly. "You're . . . I mean, he's . . . how did you find out?"

"You're babbling," Yoshiko told her.

Jenna only smiled and pleaded with her eyes.

Yoshiko shrugged. "I turned off the ringer so you wouldn't be disturbed. I checked in on you a little while ago, and Audrey had left a message. Said she owed you one, and that Danny was awake. That it was still supposed to be only family visiting, but she thought they'd let you in, 'cause Danny wants to see you."

Jenna bent over and threw her arms around Yoshiko, hugged her tight. "Oh, thank you!" she cried. "Thank God. He's going to be okay."

"Yeah, huh? Pretty cool," Yoshiko said. "Go take a shower."

"God," Jenna said, her concern turning back to her own life now that she had good news about Danny. "I had two tests today. I missed them both."

"I have a feeling they'll let you make them up," Yoshiko told her. "You have a pretty good excuse."

Jenna laughed and turned to go.

"Oh, hey, J," Yoshiko called after her.

"Yeah?"

"Have you given any thought to spring break?" Yoshiko asked, leaning forward in her chair.

Jenna stared at her. "Are you kidding? I've been a little preoccupied."

"Hunter's going home to Louisiana to spend some time with his mother," Yoshiko told her. "That leaves just you and me."

"I don't know—" Jenna began, troubled.

"Danny's going to be fine," Yoshiko replied quickly. "Here's what we're going to do. You and me, someplace tropical, away from the world, away from all this nasty stuff you keep getting into, away from school and your job, and away from corpses. Someplace where for one whole week you don't have to even think about being Action Girl, or whatever."

"But—"

"No arguments," Yoshiko said sternly.

Jenna started to reply, then shrugged and chuckled a bit. "No arguments," she agreed.

"Hey."

Danny's eyes were open and he smiled when he saw her, but he was stiff and did not turn to look at her as she walked into his room in the burn unit. There was no ventilator in the room, but he had an IV tube poking out of one arm and bandages all over his upper torso.

"Hey," he replied hoarsely. "I hear I owe you."

Jenna smiled as she took the chair next to the bed. "Nah. Audrey mostly. I helped a little, but she was the one watching over you."

"She's my partner," Danny said. "She'd better."

Despite how frail he seemed, how tentative his every word, a light danced in his eyes as though he had a new energy coursing through him. His smile was gentle, but there was also pain there.

"So, what do the doctors say?" Jenna asked.

Danny swallowed and closed his eyes when he did it, as though that simple act hurt him. When he opened them again, though, the sparkle had not left his eyes.

"I was pretty lucky, all things considered," he explained. "I've had almost no infection at all, which is a big problem with . . . with burns. I'm on a ton of antibiotics. They'll observe me for a couple of weeks, and then they'll do a graft on my stomach, where I had third-degree burns."

Jenna flinched. "Where he touched you?" she said, and heard the ache in her own voice.

"Yeah," Danny rasped.

"How long will you be here? Do they know?"

"Best case scenario, a couple of months, then in rehab for another month. Dr. Skillings thinks I'll heal up pretty well. I mean, there'll be some scars . . ." Danny let the word hang in the air and the smile disappeared from his face.

His eyes never left Jenna's, though. Not for a second.

"On my chest and my neck, they'll be visible, but not too bad. Not too noticeable. Where they do the graft, it'll be a little more so. But I'm going to be all right, Jenna. Thanks to you and Audrey, I'm going to be all right."

Jenna felt the relief wash over her.

"I'd like to visit sometimes, while you're here. Maybe I could, I don't know, read to you. A book, the newspaper, whatever. Or just, y'know, talk." She glanced away from him finally, unsure of herself.

"I'd like that," Danny replied, voice low.

Jenna smiled tentatively. She looked at his face, bright red and raw like he had a terrible sunburn. His hands were the same. He saw her looking at them and opened his right hand, laid it palm up on the edge of the bed.

"It's all right," Danny whispered. "That's a first-degree burn. It's tender, but . . . it's all right."

Heart fluttering in her chest, Jenna reached out and gently slipped her fingers into Danny's hand, held his hand in hers so gingerly. When she met his gaze again, Danny smiled.

"It's all right."

about the authors

CHRISTOPHER GOLDEN is the award-winning, *L.A. Times*–bestselling author of such novels as *Strangewood*, *Straight on 'til Morning*, and the three-volume *Shadow Saga*. His other works include *Hellboy: The Lost Army* and the Body of Evidence series of teen thrillers (including *Meets the Eye* and *Skin Deep*), which is currently being developed for television by Viacom. He has also written or cowritten a great many books, both novels and nonfiction, based on the popular TV series *Buffy the Vampire Slayer* and the world's number one comic book, *X-Men*.

Golden's comic-book work includes *Batman: Realworlds*; stints on *The Crow*, *Spider-Man Unlimited*, *Buffy the Vampire Slayer*, and *Batman Chronicles*; and the ongoing monthly *Angel* series, tying into the *Buffy* television spin-off. As a pop culture journalist, he was the editor of the Bram Stoker Award–winning book of criticism, *CUT!: Horror Writers on Horror Film*, and coauthor of both *Buffy the Vampire Slayer: The Monster Book* and *The Stephen King Universe*.

Golden was born and raised in Massachusetts,

where he still lives with his family. He graduated from Tufts University. He is currently at work on a new series for Pocket Books entitled Prowlers and a new novel for Signet called *The Ferryman*. There are more than three million copies of his books in print. Please visit him at www.christophergolden.com.

RICK HAUTALA has published eighteen books, including the million-plus-copy, international bestseller *Nightstone*, as well as *Twilight Time, Little Brothers, Beyond the Shroud, Cold Whisper,* and *Impulse*. His novel *Poltergeist: The Legacy: The Hidden Saint* (Berkley/Putnam) was published in November 1999, and a short story collection, *Bedbugs*, was published as a limited edition by CD Publications in March 2000. The year 2001 will bring the publication of two Body of Evidence novels written in collaboration with Christopher Golden. Also in 2001, his novel *The Mountain King* will be published in paperback by Leisure Books, and *The White Room* will be published under the pseudonym A. J. Matthews by Berkley Books.

Born and raised in Rockport, Massachusetts, Rick received his B.A. and M.A. in English literature from the University of Maine in Orono. He is married and lives in southern Maine with his wife and two sons. His oldest son, Aaron, is on his own, working with the progressive rock band Satellite Lot. Rick has been a full-time writer for almost twenty years.

Turn the page for a preview of
the first book in the new series

PROWLERS

by Christopher Golden
Available Spring 2001

Glass shattered.

The clientele of Bridget's Irish Rose Pub hushed for a heartbeat to glance in the general direction of the sound. A waitress had dropped a beer mug. Instantly the chatter of the crowd resumed, people tossing back pints of Guinness on draft or digging into steaming, succulent servings of shepherd's pie. Bridget's served a hell of a shepherd's pie.

Jack Dwyer hustled the short distance from the huge cooler to the long oak bar, two cases of Budweiser longnecks in his arms. The customers who came into Bridget's tended to want draft, and they tended to want it Irish import, or the next best thing. If not that, then Sam Adams. But there were still plenty of people to whom Bud was the king of beers. The longnecks were heavy, and Jack had built up considerable biceps and shoulder muscles over the years carrying kegs and cases out of the cooler. He'd never lifted weights in his life; didn't need to.

Jack only saw him in profile, but the goon standing at the end of the bar, blocking his way, didn't look at all familiar. He was maybe six feet tall, which beat Jack by an inch or two, needed a shave, and had that slack look to his features that indicated he'd had three or four too many.

"Bartender," the guy said, a little too loudly.

Over the Saturday night ruckus, nobody heard him except the twentyish couple who sat on the nearest stools waiting for a table. Bill Cantwell was down the other end, pouring a pair of pints on draft for a couple of Celtics fans with their eyes glued to the TV that was bracketed to the wall behind the bar.

"Hey!" the goon snapped. His hands were on the edge of the bar, his body almost completely around behind it now. "Bartender!"

Jack was leaning back, holding the beer cases against his body, putting the weight on his neck and shoulders. The guy was in his way.

"Excuse me," he said, loud enough, but with as little inflection as possible.

The guy rounded on him, wobbly on his feet. He glared blearily down at Jack with his lip curled back and his eyes narrowed. "Hell's your problem?"

With a sigh, Jack held in the angry retort that was on the tip of his tongue. "Just trying to get the beer through. If you'll give the bartender a second, I'm sure he'll be right with you."

The drunk snorted dismissively, turned around still blocking the way, and called out for the bartender again.

"Hey," Jack said, and he bumped the guy with the cases of beer he was carrying.

Furiously, the man turned and attempted to shove him away. Jack slid easily out of the way and the fool stumbled past him slightly. His path was now clear.

"Thanks," Jack said, a pleasant smile on his face.

"You little—" the guy began, as he reached for Jack.

"There a problem here?" a deep voice boomed.

Jack paused, let out a breath. The drunk blinked in surprise and looked past him. Bill Cantwell had finally come down the bar and stood with his big arms crossed and his bushy eyebrows pinned together above a scowl. His beard and hair were more salt than pepper these days, but he was still just as formidable a presence as when he played center for the New England Patriots fifteen years before.

"You gonna let this punk treat me like that?" the drunk sputtered. He tried to stand up straight, make himself a little more imposing in Big Bill's presence. He failed miserably.

"What do you think I should do about it?" Bill asked, amused.

The drunk liked that. Nodded to himself. "You oughta fire 'im, treatin' a customer like that. Dock his pay at least."

Bill shook his head slowly. "I don't think I can do that, my friend.

"For one, Jack's right. Only staff behind the bar and I can't serve anyone's who's obviously so drunk he probably only stumbled in here 'cause the last place stopped serving him. That'd be you. The other reason I can't do that is 'cause Jack here is one of the people who made those rules, and signs the checks. He owns fifty percent of this place."

The drunk was dumbfounded, staring at Bill in disbelief, then glancing at Jack, then back at Bill. Jack smiled.

"If I was you, I'd move on out of here without raising a fuss," Bill went on. "See, Jack wasn't kidding about throwing you out. He's a kid, sure enough, and polite as can be, just like his mother taught him, but he'll break you in half if you get up in his face. I've seen it happen."

A half-smirk still on his face, the drunk glanced doubtfully at Jack, who kept the smile on his face. But it was a cold smile, and he bounced just a bit on the balls of his feet.

Once, twice, the intoxicated fool opened his mouth to say something. At length, he turned away.

Jack raised his eyebrows and shook his head. "I don't get it," he said. "It's like they see the word *pub* and think it's somewhere they can drink 'til they puke. I mean, c'mon, have a look around. It's a nice place."

With a sigh, he looked up at Bill. "Thanks."

Bill nodded, chuckling to himself. "Anytime, tough guy. Now get the beer out of my way and into the ice before I fall over and break an arm."

"Or the floor," Jack muttered, then squeaked a protest as Bill whapped him lightly on the head. "All right, all right. Can't take a joke."

Bill went back to slinging pints and Jack started stuffing Bud longnecks into the iceboxes under the bar. He was down there on the scarred wooden floor when Courtney found him.

"Are you hiding down there, or actually working?"

The last of the Buds was stashed away, so Jack stood up and faced his sister across the bar.

"What's up?" he asked her.

Court was twenty-eight, but looked older, despite the spattering of freckles across the bridge of her nose. There were lines around her blue eyes and at the edges of her mouth, and she had cut her chestnut hair to shoulder length a few years back to save time in the mornings. On their own, Jack knew those things would not necessarily have made Courtney Dwyer look older than her age. But once you added the cane . . .

Court rapped the bar with the lion's head on her black cane; it had once belonged to their maternal grandfather, Conan Sears. "Earth to Jack. You're gonna be late."

His hands were damp from the ice and he wiped them on his pants even as his sister's words sunk in. "What? Oh, wait, what time is it?"

With a sigh, Courtney held out her watch so he could see the hands. Twenty past seven.

"Damn!" he snapped. "Artie'll be here in ten minutes."

"You'd better change, then. Don't want to be less than beautiful for dear old Artie," Courtney teased.

Jack's head spun. He glanced around the bar, then out onto the floor of the restaurant. It was busy. Waiters and waitresses hustled, faces intent, and up at the front, at least a dozen people stood waiting for tables and glaring at Wendy, the hostess on duty.

"I . . ." His voice trailed off. He glanced at

Courtney. "Are you sure you don't need me? It's pretty busy."

A look of mock horror spread across her face. "My God, Jack, I don't know," she said in a fluttery voice, with a hint of their late mother's brogue. "What do you think, Bill? Can we spare the lad for the night?"

The burly bartender topped off a pint of Bass from the tap, slid it over to a customer, then moved down the bar toward them with a patiently bemused expression on his face.

"What are you two going on about?"

"Our boy's got a hot date," Courtney told Bill.

Jack sagged against the bar. Nobody could make him feel twelve years old again the way his sister could.

"Oh really?" Bill said, puffing up his chest and crossing his arms. "And do we get to meet this girl or are you hiding her from us? Not good enough for her, are we? Or is she not good enough for us?"

"Kill me," Jack mumbled, and let his forehead slam down on the bar. He bumped it against the wood several times.

"Her name's Kate," Courtney said. "She's one of Artie and Molly's friends. Has her eye on our Jack, this Kate does."

"Can I go now?" Jack pleaded, forehead still on the bar. He could feel the grain against his skin and a damp spot where someone had set a glass not too long ago.

"I don't know if we can do without you," Courtney replied.

Jack laughed, stood up, and walked out from behind the bar. "I get it, Court. But if the place falls down on you, don't blame me."

"Be a gentleman tonight, Jack," Bill called after him.

With a shake of his head and a grin he could not hide, Jack held up his left hand and shot Bill the finger, blocking the gesture from the view of the patrons with his right. "You played professional football, buddy. I've heard about those locker rooms. Don't tell me about being a gentleman."

"Hey!" Courtney chided him for real this time. "Watch that."

His only reply was an expression of perfect who-me? innocence.

Bridget's Irish Rose Pub was two blocks away from Quincy Marketplace in downtown Boston. Once upon a time the tourists and locals who swarmed Quincy Market had seemed to exist in a kind of box, and the neighborhoods on either side were invisible beyond the walls of that box.

Over time, however, that had changed. The streets around Bridget's were cleaner, the buildings brighter, and more often than not, couples discovered the place by strolling hand in hand along the sidewalk. In reality, only a small percentage of the Quincy Market crowd wandered down that way, but it was enough to turn a once-struggling neighborhood pub into a thriving business.

As Jack changed clothes in his bedroom on the top

floor of the building he and his sister owned, he looked at the framed picture of his mother on the bureau and silently thanked her. It was a ritual for him, something he always did whenever the photo caught his eye.

Nine years she had been dead, but he still lived by Bridget Dwyer's example every day. One look around his room was testament to that. The bed was made, clothes put away, very little clutter except for the stacks of western novels ready to spill out of the little overstuffed bookshelf. His mother had taught him that if he could keep his house in order, he could keep his life in order. It was just her way of looking at the world. Sometimes it worked, sometimes it didn't, but it comforted him.

Jack's greatest regret was that she had not lived to see what her little pub had become.

"Wish me luck, Ma," he said, voice low.

With a light touch to his pockets to confirm the presence of his wallet and keys, Jack left the room. On the stairs he looked at his watch. Seven forty-five. He was running late, but not so much that Kate would be insulted. He barely knew the girl, but he didn't want her to get the wrong impression. They had met three or four times, mainly at parties, when he had been out with Artie Carroll and Artie's girl, Molly Hatcher. Kate was cute but quiet. Apparently not so quiet that it kept her from telling Molly she'd like to see more of Jack.

Not a bad thing, he thought.

It was worth a shot, anyway. Through high school,

he had never dated much because of his responsibilities to the pub and to his sister. But he'd been out almost a year now, and since school was no longer part of the equation, he figured it was time to get himself some kind of social life.

Jack was nervous. He hated it, but there was nothing he could do about it. He opened the door that led down into the restaurant, and surveyed himself one last time. A shower and a fresh shave; his bristly-short hair barely needed a brush. He wore decent-looking black boots Courtney had bought him for Christmas, a pair of Levi's, and a white T-shirt under an olive green V-neck sweater. No jacket. He wondered if it would get cold, but shrugged it off. Better to be cold than to carry it around if it was too warm.

One deep breath, then he stepped out onto the landing at the top of the steps, locked the door behind him, and went down into the maelstrom of the restaurant.

"Artie's at the bar. He's been waiting for you twenty minutes," Courtney said. "You should go before he breaks into song or convinces Bill to give him a beer just to shut him up."

Jack laughed, then turned and moved swiftly through the restaurant, dodging customers, servers, and busboys, becoming part of the ballet himself. Artie was at the far end of the bar, near the enormous frosted windows that faced the street. He was at a stool, eating popcorn from a bowl and jabbering at Bill Cantwell, who stared at Artie in a combination of amazement and dismay. More than likely, Artie was waxing poetic on one of his many favorite subjects, from gun control to the legalization of prostitution to conspiracies in the U.S. government.

Artie was something else. It wasn't really like those things meant a lot to him, he just liked to have things to talk about. To get a debate going. It had always been in his nature, but even more so since the fall, when he had begun his freshman year at Emerson College, studying broadcasting. As Jack approached, he heard Artie's rambling and knew it was gun control again. He smiled. Artie had been born and raised in downtown Boston, just like Jack. Boston Catholic High School boys. But to look at him less than a year after graduation, one would think he'd been raised in Southern California. His blond hair was long now and shaggy enough that he perpetually needed a haircut. He didn't dress like a surfer, though. It was still April in New England, after all. But the ripped, hooded BC sweatshirt he wore with jeans and battered high tops fit his new persona perfectly.

"Hey," Jack said.

Without glancing around, Artie threw a bit of popcorn over his shoulder and it hit Jack in the face. Then he turned quickly, feigning shock.

"Oh, sorry, bro. Didn't see you standing there." Artie grinned.

"Sorry I'm so late. Things just got—"

"Nuts, I know. It happens, man. Just to you more often than others. It's your life, you gotta live it. We oughta get moving, though." The way Artie spoke his sentences, they all seemed to kind of run together sometimes, like his mouth was ahead of his brain.

Jack looked around. "Where are the girls? Are we meeting them somewhere or—"

"Nah, they're double-parked across the street. Didn't think you'd be so backed up. Not that there's any parking around here anyway, right?"

"They've been outside all this time and you didn't think maybe you should tell them I was running behind?"

Artie frowned, looked at Jack as though he had been insulted. "Bro, come on. They're smart girls. They'll figure it out. We should go, though. Molly's patience isn't infinite, y'know?"

"She's in love with you," Jack replied archly. "It'd kinda have to be, wouldn't it?"

Artie punched him, slid off the stool, and turned back to Bill Cantwell, who had moved down the bar to hand a pair of sweating Budweiser longnecks to a couple of older guys waiting for a table.

"We'll have to finish our talk another time," Artie called.

"Yeah. Looking forward to it," Bill told him, with a wave and a look in his eyes usually reserved for rambling drunks and madmen.

Together, Artie and Jack walked along the frosted glass toward the front door. Jack felt surprisingly good, despite the weight of the responsibility he was shrugging off for the night. Or maybe because of it. He strolled toward the door with a calm he did not usually feel, as Artie bounced along beside him, rattling with energy as always, muttering "hey" and "how ya doin'?" to Bridget's staffers he passed, just in case he'd met them before and forgotten.

Vanilla.

Her eyes darted about, scanning the people around her as she moved along the sidewalk, on the hunt. On the prowl. Ready to spring but forcing herself to stay calm, play it cool, to lurk among the prey, unseen. Her entire body thrummed with the unreleased energy of her carnal desire, her bloodlust.

Vanilla.

Where had that scent come from? So enticingly sweet, but only the barest whiff. With a frown, Jasmine paused and lifted her nose just a bit, sniffed the air.

There.

An almost-new Toyota was parked illegally a few yards back, hazard lights blinking. The engine was not running, and the front windows were open. Through the windshield, Jasmine could see two girls. Young and tender flesh, perhaps eighteen. No more than twenty. The passenger had wild red hair, past her shoulders, and her laughter as the two girls talked was innocent and warm. The other, the driver, was colder. She was like ice to look at, with short blond hair cut in stylish waves to frame her diamond-cut features. Her voice was full of presumed knowledge and expectation.

She was Vanilla. Her natural human pheromonal scent was masked by some sort of perfume but it was not offensive to Jasmine's nose the way so many such concoctions were.

Vanilla. She looked cold but smelled sweet. And beneath the ice, the hot, raw vulnerability at the center of all humans.

Jasmine felt a tiny shudder go through her and the hairs on the back of her neck bristled with anticipation. Her flesh wanted to be released, the beast within yearning for freedom, but she focused enough to control it. Tanzer had taught her well. Her tongue snaked out and slid along her upper lip, quivering as she took a deep breath and then let it out. After another moment she crossed the dozen feet between herself and the Toyota and crouched by the passenger window.

The girls' conversation faltered and they each shot her a questioning glance.

"Hi!" Jasmine said, light and friendly.

"Hi," the passenger responded hesitantly.

Jasmine inhaled deeply of them, of Vanilla in particular, a smile on her face.

"We know you?" Vanilla asked.

"Sorry," Jasmine replied, sublimating her ancient accent as best she could. "Just a bit lost. Can you tell me how to find Quincy Market from here?"

The passenger smiled and pushed her hair behind her ears. "Yeah. You could spit on it from here. You're headed the right direction. Just . . . see right down there? You can actually see all the people? That's it."

Jasmine thanked them. The girls looked at her oddly, but she did not mind. It had been an undeniable temptation to move closer, to inhale that aroma. With a tiny, playful wave, she walked on. A moment later she glanced back to see that the girls were once again engaged in conversation and paying her no attention at all; she ducked into a narrow alley between two aging buildings. There was a fire escape there. The metal ladder was not down but she made the twelve-foot leap to grasp the bottom of the first iron landing with ease.

With a quick glance about to see that she was not being watched, Jasmine scrambled soundlessly up the fire escape to the fourth-floor landing, from which she leaped to the roof. Her muscles rolled beneath her flesh as if they had a life of their own, and there were moments as she moved that she knew her features had changed, even the texture of her skin had altered.

The beast, surging up inside her.

She shook it off and moved to the edge of the roof. From there she watched Vanilla and the other girl sit in the Toyota for another thirteen minutes until two young men, boys their own age, walked out of the pub across the street and slid into the backseat of the car. Their scents were interesting as well.

The engine roared to life, and the car began to roll off.

Jasmine pursued. She moved swiftly through the dark across the roof, darting with extraordinary speed through the nighttime shadows like nothing more than a wraith. With a grunt she leaped a sixteen-foot gap between buildings without losing a step, then continued on.

On the breeze, she scented others in her pack. She tilted her head back and uttered their ancient cry, throat ululating with it. The others responded, moving toward her across the neighborhood. Below, the car took a right turn. Jasmine sprinted to the far end of the roof and leaped out into open space, arms widespread as she fell to a roof two stories lower. She hit, went down to her knees, and rolled, then was up again in an instant and running again.

By the time her keen eyes detected others of the pack converging, two down on the ground and one on the rooftops across the street, she had already identified each of them by scent.

The gray Toyota with Vanilla behind the wheel stopped at a red light, then sped up with the flow of traffic when it turned green. Jasmine's lips curled back from spiked teeth as she put voice to the cry of the pack once more. The breeze whipped her hair and her legs pumped beneath her, carrying her at inhuman speeds across the rooftops of the city of Boston.

The hunt was on.

Look for the first book in
the exciting new series
PROWLERS
by Christopher Golden
Available from Pocket Books
April 2001

They're real, and they're here...

When Jack Dwyer's best friend Artie is murdered, he is devastated. But his world is turned upside down when Artie emerges from the ghostlands to bring him a warning.

With his dead friend's guidance, Jack learns of the Prowlers. They move from city to city, preying on humans until they are close to being exposed, then they move on.

Jack wants revenge. But even as he hunts the Prowlers, he marks himself—and all of his loved ones—as prey.

Don't miss the exciting new series from

BESTSELLING AUTHOR CHRISTOPHER GOLDEN!

PROWLERS

POCKET PULSE

PUBLISHED BY POCKET BOOKS

3083

"I'm the Idea Girl, the one who can always think of something to do."

VIOLET EYES

A spellbinding new novel of the future

by Nicole Luiken

Angel Eastland knows she's different. It's not just her violet eyes that set her apart. She's smarter than her classmates and more athletically gifted. Her only real competition is Michael Vallant, who also has violet eyes—eyes that tell her they're connected, in a way she can't figure out.

Michael understands Angel. He knows her dreams, her nightmares, and her most secret fears. Together they begin to realize that nothing around them is what it seems. Someone is watching them, night and day. They have just one desperate chance to escape, one chance to find their true destiny, but their enemies are powerful—and will do anything to stop them.

Available from

Published by Pocket Books   3074

. . . A GIRL BORN
WITHOUT THE FEAR GENE

FEARLESS™

A SERIES BY
FRANCINE PASCAL

POCKET
PULSE

FROM POCKET PULSE
PUBLISHED BY POCKET BOOKS

3029

Everyone's got his demons....

ANGEL™

If it takes an eternity, he will make amends.

Original stories based
on the TV show
Created by Joss Whedon
& David Greenwalt

Available from Pocket Pulse
Published by Pocket Books

2311-01